About the author

The recipient of the YCOF National Excellence Award and the winner of the National Debut Youth Fiction Award 2013, Faraaz Kazi is also called as the Nicholas Sparks of India. A digital entrepreneur and a three-time post-grad, Kazi has previously authored three bestselling titles in India – *Truly Madly Deeply* (2010), *The Other Side* (2013) and *LOVE* (2015).

Kazi is a fellow member of the esteemed Film Writers Association of India and an active member of The International Horror Writers Association. *Truly Madly Deeply*, his debut mainstream romance novel, is the only Indian book to be nominated in seven categories of the Goodreads annual choice awards, apart from being the first Indian novel to win the 'Best Debut (Romance)' during the same awards. It is also the only Indian book in the 'Top 100 YA Global Fiction' list. *The Other Side*, which Kazi co-authored with Vivek Banerjee, remains the highest selling Indian horror title till date. Kazi is a voracious reader and counts singing as his second love.

You can reach him on Facebook, Twitter and Instagram @FaruKazi.

About the author

Meant to be Together

Faraaz Kazi

Srishti
PUBLISHERS & DISTRIBUTORS

Srishti Publishers & Distributors
Registered Office: N-16, C.R. Park
New Delhi – 110 019
Corporate Office: 212A, Peacock Lane
Shahpur Jat, New Delhi – 110 049
editorial@srishtipublishers.com

First published as a digital book by
Juggernaut Books in 2016

Revised version, 2019
First Published by
Srishti Publishers & Distributors in 2019

10 9 8 7 6 5 4 3 2 1

This is a work of fiction. The characters, places, organisations and events described in this book are either a work of the author's imagination or have been used fictitiously. Any resemblance to people, living or dead, places, events, communities or organisations is purely coincidental.

Printed and bound in India

Dedicated to all those memories
that we could never wipe off.

In the room with the pale blue walls, the woman mumbles incoherently under her breath, feverishly turning the pages of a bulky photo album that rests on her lap. Her eyes are swollen; her demeanour like a beast that has finally broken free from its shackles after spending a lifetime in captivity.

She pushes her handbag away, its contents spilling all over the bed – a kohl stick, a pack of tissues, a toffee, some loose change and a dozen visiting cards with 'Preeti Thaker, IT Manager, Obsoft' printed on them She doesn't bother putting them back. The album nestled on her lap, legs stretched out in front of her and back slouched over, Preeti sways back and forth examining each photograph. She gingerly traces the figures in them, the veins in her hands gleaming like raging tributaries.

The air in the room suddenly grows thick with melancholy. She is transfixed by a photograph of a teenage boy wearing a loose shirt and shorts, his hand resting on the shoulders of a little girl wearing a red polka-dotted frock. Happiness is etched on their faces. She stares at it for several moments before taking it out from the plastic film that covers it. She holds it with the affection of a mother for her newborn child, tender and loving.

Preeti's eyes soften briefly. The lava of hurt makes its way into her throat, setting ablaze all that she has held within. Her tears smear the photograph, a silent spectator.

Her sleep-deprived eyes ache in protest as she devours the same pictures again and again. Her stomach protests too; the stale slices of bread she had for dinner the previous evening – the only thing in her refrigerator that had not gone bad – were obviously not enough.

The apartment reeks of paint and nicotine. The heavy navy blue curtains drawn tightly across stand guard, not letting any sunlight filter into the room. The only light in the room comes from the white clinical glow of a CFL bulb.

The apartment is a mess. Empty canvases, paintbrushes with matted tips and tubes of acrylic paint lie scattered on the floor under the window. A white easel stands in the corner with a canvas mounted on it, a few careless strokes of red and orange on its crest. Dozens of painted canvases are stacked up untidily against the wall; silent witnesses to the happenings of the past seventy-two hours.

Preeti wraps her arms around her knees and buries her head in them. Sleep has evaded her for long and her eyes close of their own volition. She emerges out of the daze a few minutes later wearing a forlorn, defeated look. She turns her head towards the window to the left. Just where the mattress meets the wall lies a stack of diaries.

Preeti looks at them vacantly, lost in her thoughts. After a long time, she crawls on her knees and picks up the oldest looking diary from the lot. Returning to her former position, she wipes its dust-covered pink jacket on her black T-shirt and props it up against her folded legs. The moment she opens it, a few dried leaves fall on her lap.

The pages are full of untidy doodles. The handwriting in pencil is barely legible – clearly the work of a child. She carefully places the leaves aside and starts reading.

The life of a happy child unfolds before Preeti's eyes. The little girl who has written this diary seems to lead a charmed life: a close-knit family, parents who dote on her and fulfil her every wish, however unreasonable. The entries are full of details of her dolls, her frocks, her umpteen toy-houses and everything that could possibly matter to a child. The initial entries offer a glimpse into a beautiful, innocent world, untouched by the remotest shadow of grief. She reads on.

1/4/1990

papa give me this book
it is pink. i like the flowr on it. it hs so mny flowr
i love papa.

◆

12/10/1990

i hate papa.
he wont play cach with me. mama say he cant walk.
papa spoil my birday. i hate him

Preeti glances over the entry again and shakes her head. She lights another cigarette. Bookmarking the page with her index finger, the memory of that day, faint but persistent, floats back to her.

"Beta, papa can't walk anymore! He can't play catch with you like he used to."

"But why?" asked the little girl as she stared at her mother in anger, tears streaming down her face.

"Because he can't get up from the bed, beta!"

"Lie, lie, lie! You are lying!" she screamed, stomping her feet on the floor.

"Beta, your mama is not lying. I can't walk..." her father tried to explain.

"Papa is just lazy. You're all lying!" she yelled looking around the room.

Her mother, grandmother and brother, Hitesh, wore solemn expressions on their faces, trying hard not to break down.

"And I hate you all! I hate you, papa!"

She picked up her yellow sponge ball that lay on the floor near the foot of the hospital bed, flung it at her bedridden father and stormed out of the room. Hitesh ran after his sister calling out her name.

"She is too young to understand, Pulkit. Give her some time..." the little girl's mother said to her husband between tears as her husband wept quietly on the bed.

Pulkit Thaker, a customs and excise officer working in Baroda, and a well-known figure in political circles, had met with an accident on his daughter's sixth birthday as he made his way home from office with her favourite black forest cake for her party. The birthday cake never arrived home, but a year later, Pulkit Thaker did, paralysed from the waist down.

◆

5/11/1990

i dont want to go

i dont want to leave mama and go. nani love hitu more

i miss old papa a lot. i pray to god papa walk again.

◆

"Hitesh beta, take care of your sister," said Aarti stroking her son's hair gently.

"Yes mama, I will."

The little girl sat at the back of the car, arms folded across her chest, tears in her eyes and head bowed. She was furious with her mother and had not spoken to her since the previous evening. A huge chocolate bar lay in her lap. On any other day, she would have already eaten it. She occasionally raised her head and looked at her home: a pristine white bungalow with a manicured garden in the front. A giant mango tree stood in one corner of the garden. She wondered how long it would be before she could play on the giant swing that hung from it again.

"Help her with her homework, check on her while you are in school..." Aarti told her son while looking at her daughter, hoping she would turn around and look at her.

"Mama, please don't worry. I will take care of everything. You just take care of papa, he needs you."

"My brave, brave boy," she said, her lips quivering. She kissed her son on the forehead and hugged him tightly. "I love you two so much... I feel terrible that your papa and I are not going to be around for you two as much as we would want to," she said between sobs.

After struggling for weeks, trying to split her hours between taking care of her husband in the hospital and spending time with her children at home, Aarti felt that her children were being neglected. Sending them away to her mother's place in a distant part of the town was the only viable and sensible option left.

"Bye baby! I love you!" said Aarti, opening the side door and kissing her daughter's head. Hitesh was now sitting beside her, trying to persuade her to talk to their mother, but she refused to listen.

"I am sorry, sweetheart! I am so sorry." Aarti apologized to her daughter and shut the door as the driver revved up the engine.

"Bye mama!" said Hitesh.

The little girl sniffed,her tears tap-tapping softly on to the chocolate packet on her lap.

Once the car disappeared from view, Aarti walked towards the swing and sat on it, burying her face in her hands. The swing responded to her sobs, rocking her back and forth as if it was trying to calm her down.

◆

15/11/1990

nani made karela today.yuck!
mama never give me karela.
i miss mama's food.
nani call mama today.
i and hitu talk to her
we also talk to papa.
i miss them so much.

◆

17/12/1990

nani cant tie my hair like mama.
i ask hitu and he made it nice.
i miss mama and papa.
i miss our house.
nani says god fix every thing.
please god fix every thing with femicol glu
hitu say femicol glu very strong, nothing can brake it
god tie me, hitu and mama and papa with femicol glu.

◆

19/12/1990

god please panish hina garima sheetal. I hate them and make papa walk.

◆

"...and then papa took me and Hitesh for a ride on the giant wheel."

"But my mummy told me that your papa can't walk..." Hina interrupted.

"Liar, liar! Pants on fire!" Garima and Sheetal teased her in a sing-song voice and all three of them laughed.

Tears streaming down her face, the little girl screamed, "No, no, no! Hina's mummy is a liar. My papa can walk. Hina's mummy is very bad, she lies."

But all three girls continued to point fingers at her and laugh harder seeing her reaction. The little girl ran away, vowing never to speak to them again.

◆

5/1/1991

rosie miss ask to me to put my hands up.
i fail math test.
every one laugh at me hina sheetal garima akhil every one
rosie miss write me note in book.
she say that papa must sign it
i dont want to go skool.

◆

"You got a big fat zero in your test. Do you want to stay in this class for another year? Your final exams are going to start in three months. What are you going to do?" Miss Rosie thundered, waving the paper in the air.

The class burst into quiet sniggers.

"How many times do we have to discuss the same things in class? We must have done these sums a hundred times at least!" she said and slammed the paper on the table in frustration.

She picked up a piece of chalk, walked over to the board and scribbled '5+3'. Then she handed the chalk to the little girl and stood next to her with her arms folded, a stern look etched on her face.

The little girl started counting feverishly on her fingers. Her ears were burning up. She solved the sum several times, each time coming up with a different answer, writing it on the board and then erasing it with the palm of her hand. After several minutes and much hesitation, she wrote her final answer.

"Five plus three is six. Excellent!" Miss Rosie remarked sarcastically.

"Wrong ma'am!" the class said in unison. Several students raised their hands, calling out to Miss Rosie, trying to get her attention.

"Shhh!" the teacher hissed at the class. "Can you tell us how you got that answer?" she asked the little girl.

"Yes ma'am," she responded meekly, nodding her head. The little girl put the chalk in the little grey cardboard box near the board, wiped her dusty hands on her olive green skirt and started counting aloud, holding out one finger with each count. When she finished counting till seven, she was holding up six fingers: five on her left hand and a thumb on the right.

"Wrong! Wrong!" several voices shouted.

"Ma'am, can I write the answer?"

"Ma'am, I know the answer." Nearly half the class was now on their feet. Amid the chaos, someone prompted from the back of the class: "Five plus three is eight!"

"Everyone sit down and be quiet!" Miss Rosie shouted.

But no one was willing to listen. As she tried to gain control of her class, the little girl quickly picked up a piece of chalk and twisted the top of the six that she had already scribbled on the board and changed it to an eight. The entire class broke into laughter.

Miss Rosie, unaware of what had just happened behind her back, slapped her hands on one of the desks in the front row and yelled, "Enough! If I see anyone laughing, or talking, or getting up from their benches now, he or she will go straight to the principal's office."

The class fell silent. Then she turned around to look at the little girl who was now holding up eight fingers. "Who told you the answer?" Miss Rosie barked at her, spraying her face with spit.

"No one, ma'am."

"Then why was your first answer incorrect?"

"But it was half right, ma'am!"

Miss Rosie's eyes flashed dangerously. "Don't try to act smart! I am going to write a note in your diary. Get it signed by your father and tell your parents to meet me first thing in the morning day after tomorrow."

◆

As the entries unfold, Preeti realizes that the little girl did well in all subjects in school, except one: Mathematics. Numbers didn't make any sense to her. They were like a whirlpool of gibberish to her nubile mind. After getting an earful from the teacher and standing outside the class the first two times for not getting the note signed by her father, the little girl started getting her notes signed by her grandmother. It infuriated her teacher, who was unaware she lived with her grandmother and thought the girl was being sly.

Getting punished and humiliated in front of the class day after day became an acceptable routine for her. She never explained her situation, that her parents could not sign her notes, because getting punished seemed a better alternative to revealing the truth and being bullied daily by her classmates.

◆

17/1/1991
Mama papa wont come for my dance on friday.
i hate them.
they dont love me
hina garima mama papa come to skool.
My dont.

◆

"Garima, you were great, honey! We are so proud of you!" said Garima's mother as she kissed her daughter on the forehead.

Garima and seven other girls from her class danced to a popular number at the annual school function. The little girl was a part of the group. After the performance,she waited all by herself backstage while the other girls were surrounded by their family members. She could hear all the parents gushing over their children's performances. She wanted her parents to tell her that she was great too, to fuss over her and pamper her.

Garima was wearing a white frock with lace trims and a sparkling tiara. Large thermocol wings shaped like a butterfly's were strapped to her back. The little girl looked at Garima's wings with envy. Her parents had spent around three hours cutting them out and decorating them, Garima had proudly announced before the dance began. The little girl's wings looked like they belonged to a diseased bat. Their grandmother had fallen ill a week before the annual function, so Hitesh had taken over the responsibility of helping his sister put together everything for her dance. He had done the best that he could.

"Chutki!" Hitesh yelled, standing in the wings. The little girl waved at her brother and ran towards him, eager to get out of there, partly embarrassed by her shoddy appearance, partly sick of hearing everyone praise their children when her own parents were missing.

"Chutki, you were the best!" said Hitesh grinning from ear to ear.

"Thank you, Hitu!"

"This is for you," he said, handing her a big bar of chocolate, which he had bought for her with his pocket money.

"Thank you, Hitu! I love you!" she said, wrapping her arms around her brother's waist.

◆

23/2/1991

today is father dotter day in school.
papa cant go.
i dont want to go to school.
my frends make fun of me.
nani force me.

◆

"Why...why did you send me to school, nani? Why?" asked the little girl. "I told you everyone will tease me," she wailed.

"Beta, what happened?"

"Deepesh said that it was father-daughter day. He said your father is not here, why did you come to school? Then everyone laughed at me," she sniffed noisily and blew her nose on the sleeve of her white shirt. "It's all your fault, nani! All your fault!"

"Beta, they are all fools, don't listen to them..."

"You say that all the time, nani! Everyone makes fun of me. Everyone took part in the three-legged race. Amit says to everyone that her papa can only take part in a no-leg race. No one talks to me nicely. All because of papa…even the teachers punish me everyday. I don't want to go to school. I hate everyone!" she cried. She picked up her water bottle and threw it against the wall. The cap cracked and fell off.

"Chutki…" said Hitesh in a soothing voice and put his hand on her shoulder.

The little girl pushed him away. "I want mama papa. I won't live here." She screamed as loud as she could.

"Beta, calm down, what will the neighbours think?"

"I want mama papa right now! Now!"

"Beta, you know that is not possible. Papa is lying in a hospital bed, unable to walk, and mama is taking care of him. And they are far away from us."

"I pray to god that I also have an accident like papa. Then mama will take me with her and take care of me," she said and ran off to her room.

◆

Over the next few entries, it becomes clear that the little girl relied on her brother for everything. He seemed to be her mother, father and friend. He answered all her questions and listened patiently to her endless rants, all of which she mentions in broken sentences to her only other confidante –her diary. Like a parent, Hitesh encouraged her to keep trying when she wanted to give up and praised her when she did something well. But Hitesh, after all, was just six years older than her, and despite his best intentions and efforts, didn't manage to completely fill the void of parental love in the little girl's life.

The little girl continued to struggle with maths. She had been called 'dumb nut' so often, she now called herself that, eyeing her classmates with hatred. Envy is a natural by-product when your childhood isn't the way it is supposed to be, like that of others her age, her classmates.

Preeti closes the journal and picks up the next. By now, it is clear to her that as the little girl grew older, she went deeper and deeper into her shell. While the other kids in the neighbourhood played hide-and-seek in the evening or went cycling, she spent most of her time holed up in her room, playing by herself, drawing or writing in her diary. Even in school, she wrote in her diary, often sitting by herself in the classroom and eating lunch alone during the break. It was only when she started skipping meals and began to return her tiffin uneaten for a week that Hitesh realized what was happening. An entry highlights how Hitu got cross with her for not having her food. From the day after the discovery, Hitesh started accompanying his sister during lunch everyday, all the while encouraging her to mingle with her classmates. If due to some reason or the other, he failed to go to her class during lunchtime, the little girl's tiffin remained untouched.

The little girl seemed to have two distinct personalities. Outside the house, she seems shy and timid, but around her family members, she assumes a completely different personality. At home, everyone struggled to come to terms with her difficult behaviour. Hell bent on having her way, she threw tantrums over trivial things, made unreasonable demands and created a ruckus if they were not fulfilled. She was eager for attention, that much was evident to Preeti, who was engrossed by the little girl's tale and completely oblivious to her own state.

◆

17/4/1992
Hitu is going to bording school. What will I do?
I feel lost. I feel sad.
I am going to miss him.

◆

Hitesh tops his tenth standard board exams in school. His parents and teachers feel that given the right guidance, he can flourish. So it is decided that he will be sent to the best college in the state.

◆

"Chutki, don't skip lunch just because I'm not around," Hitesh told his sister.

The little girl's eyes were brimming with tears. She simply nodded her head. They were at the bus stop. Aarti was also there to see off her son. She stood with her arms wrapped around her daughter's shoulders protectively.

"...and don't believe anyone who tells you that you are a dumb nut, okay? Don't give up if you fail, keep trying...once, twice, thrice...just don't give up, no matter how many tries it takes. Chutki, are you even listening to me?"he asked and hugged her.

"Don't go, Hitu, please!"she wailed. "First mama, then papa, now you...you all are leaving me."

Hitesh knelt down and put his hands on her sister's shoulders. "I am always there for you, Chutki. So are mama and papa. I am only going away for some time. I will come back during my school vacations, I promise," he said.

"Pinky promise?" the girl asked, wiping her tears.

"Pinky promise," Hitesh said and wrapped his pinky finger around hers.

◆

As Preeti reads on, she realizes that Hitesh's departure seems to have benumbed the little girl's senses and arrested her thoughts. Preeti understands that it is her brother who picked her up every time she fell, held her hand and walked with her, fighting her uncertainties and fears alongside her. He is the only family she had. When he left, the wounds that they had fixed together get ripped open again, bringing her back to square one.

Her loneliness seems to get worse. There were days when she wanted to run away from home. It is clear to Preeti that the little girl had lost all interest in studies. School had become a nightmare, especially now that her brother was no longer around to give her company during lunch breaks and listen to her.

She seemed to have become impervious to things that once rattled her. She understood that no matter how much she cried and prayed to god to make things right, nothing was going to happen – her father was never going to walk again and she was never going to stay with her parents and brother like a normal family. Her parents and grandmother thought that she had matured. In reality, she had given up on everything. She seemed to have accepted her life, finally!

◆

13/7/1992

It was Garima's birthday on Monday. She calld me for her birthday party.

There was Sheetal, Abhinav, Sailee and monkey Mahesh.

There was cake and baloons. Everyone was dancing.

Garima's parents give her gifts.

Monkey Mahesh made fun of me when I dance. I ignore him.

I will be 9 next month.
I want a birthday party too with baloons and cakes.

◆

"Happy birthday, beta!" said the little girl's grandmother, affectionately planting a kiss on her granddaughter's forehead.

"Thank you, nani," she said. She yawned noisily and snuggled into her blanket. "Where is my gift, nani?" she asked eagerly.

Her grandmother laughed and pulled out a beautifully wrapped box from under the bed. "This is for my precious darling!" she said.

The little girl sprang up and started opening the wrapping paper. Inside was a beautiful red frock with frills and lace. "I love it, nani! Can I wear it to school today?" she asked, jumping off the bed with the frock in her hand.

"Careful... of course, you can! And I have also got chocolates for your classmates..."

"Nani, how do I look?" she asked before her grandmother could finish her sentence. She was holding the frock close to herself and admiring her reflection in the dressing table mirror.

"You look like a princess!"

"Nani, when is mama coming?" she asked, laying the frock down carefully on the bed. She continued, "Nani, do you remember Garima's birthday? I was thinking that..."

"Beta, mama won't be coming today," she said quietly.

"But she promised me last month that she was going to come for my birthday this time..."

"Beta, your papa has fever...mama has to take care of him," she said.

The truth was that Pulkit was undergoing a critical surgery that day, but she didn't want to upset her grandchild.

"Nani, then we can go there after I come back from school."

"Beta, that isn't possible either. Your mama has..."

"Okay," she said with nonchalance, suppressing her anger.

"Beta, you were saying something before..."

"Nothing, nani. I am going to brush my teeth now. There's no need to get that blackforest cake. I don't need this frock. I'll wear my old one to school," she said and carelessly flung the frock on the bed before walking away.

◆

Preeti is lying on the mattress, staring blankly at the roof. The diary rests on her chest. She reaches for the cigarette packet, not taking her gaze off the lone bug that is crawling on the ceiling. She gets hold of the packet after several minutes, but realizes it is empty. In the past few hours, her stomach has stopped growling but it still demands food in weaker protests. Preeti can't muster the energy to get up and scavenge for food in the kitchen. She peels her eyes off the insect and opens another diary.

◆

5/10/1994

I heard nani talk to mama today on phone. She complains that I don't speak much. And stay locked up in my room all day. I feel so scared now. I wish to disappear and not live with it and face it every day. But I have to, and that hurts.

◆

The little girl had stopped talking to her grandmother completely. Her grandmother had to ask her something several times before receiving a monosyllabic answer. She refused to sleep alone at night and insisted on keeping all the lights switched on at all times. She had always hated going to school, but now she seemed terrified at the prospect. Earlier, Math was the only subject she struggled with; now she was failing in all her subjects. Her grandmother tried to find out what is bothering her, but she refused to say anything. Since the change in her behaviour started nearly a year-and-a-half after Hitesh's departure, it was obvious that something else was bothering her.

◆

3/11/1994

Hitu has been trying to be very sweet to me since he got back here for the Diwali vacations.

I had promised myself that I won't tell my secret to anyone, not even to Hitu, but I don't know... once he started talking to me, I just told him my secret anyway. He didn't yell at me. He didn't say that it was my fault. I feel a little better now.

◆

"Chutki, you've made so many new ones since the last time I saw your book!" Hitesh exclaimed. He was looking at his sister's sketchbook.

"Hmm," she said absentmindedly, biting into the chocolate bar her brother had got her.

Most of her drawings were about her family: her mother, father, grandmother, Hitesh and herself, standing in front of a house holding hands, celebrating festivals together, going to beaches and fairs and being everything that they were not. There were drawings of mountains and rivers, rainbows and butterflies. They looked like the artwork of a regular ten-year-old, slightly more gifted, if anything. Then Hitesh started noticing an unsettling pattern in the sketches she had drawn over the past two months.

A deformed, hideous, demon-like character with horns had started appearing in her sketches consistently. The figure appeared alongside a little girl. In one sketch, the little girl cowered in terror while the demon stood over her. Hitesh assumed that the demon in the paintings was his sister's way of expressing her insecurities. But as he continued looking at the sketches, he noticed that they were becoming increasingly disturbing and he was forced to rethink his initial assumption.

The demon seemed to be pulling at the girl's skirt in one sketch. In another sketch, the girl lay on the floor of a classroom, curled up in a foetal position while the demon laughed. In another one, the demon was lying on top of the sleeping girl.

"Chutki, is this you?" he asked, pointing at the girl in the sketch.

"Hmm..."

"And who is this?" he asked, pointing at the demon.

"A monster," she replied, her eyes filling up with tears.

"Chutki," he said in a soothing voice and put his arms around his sister, "is there something that you want to share with me?"

"No..." her voice nearly cracked.

"Chutki? What's the matter?"

"Nothing."

"Chutki? Did someone hurt you? Chutki?"

She simply stared at her hands.

"Chutki, look at me."

The little girl froze for a moment and then looked up at her brother, her lower lip quivering, tears flowing down her cheeks. The next instant she buried her face in her brother's chest and began to howl. Hitesh tried his best to soothe her.

After several minutes, she looked up and said, "Hitu...Hitu, he touched me...my, my PT teacher, Jacob sir..."

Hitesh paused for a moment, reigning in his anger. "Preeti, my Chutki...he won't do it again, I promise," he said, stroking her hair.

◆

Preeti slams the journal shut, her shoulders shaking in agony as the painful memories of her early childhood take over her thoughts. The little girl has grown up to be a fine young woman – a young woman plagued by a past that won't let her live her present. A young woman called Preeti Thaker.

Preeti rocks back and forth with her arms wrapped around herself. She tries to overcome the emotions unleashed by the memories she had hitherto confined to the back of her mind. She looks blankly at the innocuous stack of diaries, their appearance so deceiving. Her wounds still raw and burning, she picks up another diary, ready to submerge herself again. She can't disown her past, neither can she run away from it. However hideous and lacerated and painful it is, reliving it brings a sense of catharsis to her aching heart.

◆

4/2/1995

I feel scared all the time. I feel like HE is still watching me, about to pounce on me anytime. Every time a boy looks at me, I feel like he is going to do to me what sir did. I don't trust anyone. And I feel...I feel dirty. I wish I could shed my skin wherever he touched me. I scrub so hard when I bathe, but he still hides under my skin. It burns. Nani told me about hell once. I think this is it.

◆

"Nani!" Preeti screamed.

It was three in the morning and she had woken up from a nightmare, shivering like a leaf caught in tumultuous winds, beads of cold sweat trickling down the back of her neck. She had been haunted by the same nightmare for months now. A shadow chased her down a dark alley until she had nowhere to run; with her back against the wall, her shoulders pinned by its icy touch, she would meet the eyes of the shadow only to see empty sockets and a crooked grin on its face, blood trickling down its teeth.

"Chutki," her grandmother said reassuringly as she came running into the brightly lit room. "I am here, Chutki...don't worry, everything is fine," she said cradling her head in her arms.

"Nani, it was that nightmare again..." she sobbed and buried her head in her grandmother's lap.

"Chutki, you have to be strong, you have to fight your fears, I can't do it for you, no one can. I know it's tiring and scary, but you have to fight," she said stroking her granddaughter's hair.

◆

19/4/1995

I am so happy Hitu is back! I have waited so long for his junior college to get over! Now he can stay here with us and study. Nani, Hitu and I went to see mama and papa on Saturday. Papa looked weaker than last time, but he still tries to do his office work while lying in bed.

Mama told me some strange things about growing up and how things were going to change from now on. She spoke about boys and the thing that I am going to get every month...I felt so icky.

I don't understand why all the girls in my class make such a big fuss about boys. I don't feel comfortable around them.

◆

17/7/1995

I am missing mama a lot today. Our English teacher asked us to write an essay on 'my mother' a week ago. She asked us to read out our essays in class today. Himani talked about how her mother cooks her favourite food when she gets good marks in her exams. Natasha said that her mother paints her toenails. Vineeta said that her mother always wipes her tears when she is sad. And Ajay said that his mother beats him when he does something naughty.I ended up submitting a blank sheet. I just couldn't bring myself to write anything.

◆

7/9/1997

I don't get time to write much these days. I spend most of my time studying. Math is so tough in eighth standard. Every time I think about giving up, Hitu is right there by my side.

◆

"I didn't understand, Hitu," said Preeti flatly.

"We've been solving the same questions for the past six days, Preeti! And you still can't solve this sum. It's the simplest problem in this exercise! You need to find the area of a parallelogram. All the data is given. It can't get any simpler than that! This isn't seventh standard anymore. In two years, you will be sitting for the board exams. You need to put in more effort, Preeti!" Her brother was exasperated.

Preeti's eyes welled up. Hitesh had always been very supportive and patient with his little sister. He rarely raised his voice or got angry with Preeti.

"Hitu, why are you yelling at me?" she asked, tears streaming down her plump cheeks.

"Preeti, don't expect everyone to pamper you all the time. You're no longer a child. Think about your future. What will you do if you fail your board exams?" he asked angrily.

"Hitu... I try, I really do! Don't be angry with me. I will study harder. I promise!"she said crying.

Hitesh felt guilty for having lost his cool. He pulled his sister towards himself and hugged her tightly. "I am sorry, Chutki, I am really sorry."

◆

11/11/1998

We went to see mama and papa today. They saw my half-yearly exam results. I was so embarrassed. But they didn't yell at me for scoring poorly in math. They were kind and encouraging. It means so much to have their support, but I know it's not going to make me smarter overnight. I feel guilty for letting them down time and again. I wonder if they will ever feel about me the way they feel about Hitu. I wonder if I'll ever be able to give them a reason to be proud of me.

◆

12/6/1999

Tenth standard is as scary as everyone makes it out to be. I do not understand anything – geometry, algebra, sin theta, alpha, beta – nothing. What will I do? I feel like a loser. Hitu is so clever and good at everything, I wish I was like him. Everyone in class keeps discussing about what they are going to do after the board exams, which colleges they are going to apply to...and all I can think of is just passing the exams.

◆

29/12/1999

Just a few more months to go before the board exams start. I have only completed the first two chapters of the math syllabus till now. Hitu has been teaching me math for two hours every day for three months now. He has also made a timetable for me to follow.

Mama calls me frequently these days. She is always trying to motivate me. But I know I am going to let all of them down. How will I face them if I fail? What about college? Hitu went to the best college, and I will end up going to a college attended by students who get bad scores. My family will be so ashamed of me.

◆

3/3/2000

There are only three math chapters that I have understood till now, and judging by the previous year's papers, they don't carry any weightage. I am not going to be able to finish the syllabus in time. There is no way I am sitting for the Math exam. I would much rather be absent than fail. If I tell anyone at home they will not allow me to skip the exam. Maybe I won't go to the exam centre that day... Maybe I'll tell Hitu...

◆

"Hitu, this doesn't feel right..."

"Preeti," said Hitesh angrily, "you said you couldn't sit for the exam. This is the only way out so stop complaining. You are lucky that mama and papa agreed to do this..."

"Hitu, I am sorry, please don't be angry with me..." She tugged at her brother's arms.

"Preeti, just write the paper now, Mehta uncle is waiting in the living room to collect it after three hours," he said tersely, pushing a thin file in her direction. It was the Math question paper.

◆

12/3/2000

The Math exam is over. I feel so relieved! I am going to pass, but I feel so guilty. Had there been another way, I would have taken it.

◆

2/6/2000

I passed my boards in first class. Still can't believe it! Nani and I visited papa in the hospital today. Even now, he continues to do his office work though he is bedridden. He is such an inspiration.

◆

"Papa!" exclaimed Preeti as she ran towards her father.

As they hugged, Aarti walked into the room accompanied by a nurse. After greeting each other and congratulating Preeti, everyone settled down for a chat. Despite Preeti's best efforts, the conversation steered towards the plan for her future. She could feel the heat rising to her ears; she couldn't meet anyone's eyes even though the subject of her math exam never came up.

"Preeti, it's okay, beta, forget about it," said her mother, reading her daughter's mind. "It's done, beta, there is no point feeling guilty now. The important thing is what you are going to do in the future and how well you do it."

Touched by her family's unshakeable faith in her, Preeti's eyes welled up. She stammered, "I…I am sorry, mama…I am so, so sorry, papa, I am sorry, nani…I really tried… forgive me…"

Aarti held her daughter and consoled her: "Shh…it's okay, beta, no one is angry with you."

Preeti's grandmother and father had similar words of kindness and encouragement; everyone was upset, but they also understood that Preeti needed their unflinching support.

"I am so sorry...I, I don't want to study anymore, mama... I don't want to do this again, mama," she cried, tightening her grip around her mother's waist.

"Preeti," her mother said lovingly as she cupped her daughter's face in her hands.

"Look at your papa, Preeti. Have you ever seen him give up? No! Never! After all these years...had it been someone else, perhaps he would have given up on life a long time ago, but not your father. You are his daughter, Preeti, and you have the same spirit, I know it! I see it in you. You can't give up! I know it is difficult for you, but you need to keep moving ahead, just like your father. Don't let anything set you back in life, beta... do you hear me?"

Preeti looked at her mother and nodded.

Her mother continued, "I know you will make us proud one day, just like your brother has. Put all your doubts aside. You are going to study further, pursue science and then opt for engineering."

Even though she nodded, fear plagued her as she realized that this was merely the beginning of her struggles. Deep down, she wanted to give up, but she knew that she had already let her family down once and she couldn't do it again.

◆

12/8/2000

I thought tenth standard was tough but eleventh is tougher! I am going insane handling physics and chemistry in addition to my old enemy math. It's my worst nightmare... numbers everywhere... what the hell have I gotten myself into?

◆

6/4/2001

It has been a long time since I wrote anything... these last few months have been awfully strenuous. I have studied harder than ever. I got my results today. I failed. This is humiliating. I didn't want to come home today. Hitu, nani, mama and papa were all very kind. I could tell they were disappointed, but they didn't say anything. I wish they got angry with me and screamed at me. At least that way I would have a reason to put an end to my pathetic life. But they give me so much love despite my failures that it makes me want to keep trying.

◆

16/5/2003

I passed my twelfth standard board exams! I did it! I can't believe it! I scored 58%! I know it may not mean much to anyone, but this is a huge accomplishment. I owe it to Hitu, had it not been for him, I would have never made it this far. Not in my wildest dreams did I see this day coming. I will be starting college in a few months! Who would have thought I would ever go to college! I feel so nervous and excited at the same time!

◆

23/7/2003

Everything seems so different in college. It's like a completely new world. I'm not sure if I like it: too many people, too much of everything! I still have to keep pinching myself to believe that this is happening. How did I make it this far?

◆

"Hi! I am Vipul. Will you dance with me?"

"Umm, no, I don't dance, thanks anyway," said Preeti and smiled awkwardly.

She was at the fresher's party,dressed in a burgundy silk dress that ended right above her knees. She had left her jet black curly hair loose so that her luscious curls skimmed her shoulders. With her flawless face, almond-shaped dark brown eyes and just a touch of pink on her lips, she was the cynosure of all eyes. While the dance floor brimmed with young couples, Preeti stood quietly in a corner, occasionally fixating over random people who caught her attention for no specific reason. After an hour of waiting and watching, she called her brother.

"Hitu, can you come and pick me up?"

"So soon? Is it over?"

"Yeah," she lied.

◆

13/9/2003

I failed in all the subjects in the first semester. I can't keep going anymore. I am sick of trying and failing repeatedly. I wonder what my life holds for me... or if it holds anything at all.

◆

"Preeti, it's four in the morning! Come on now, go to bed! That's three days in a row, Chutki! You will fall ill..." said her grandmother as she walked into her bedroom.

"Nani, please... I need to study. I can't fail again," she said stifling her yawn. The dark circles under her eyes told the story of the sleepless nights she had spent studying.

◆

"What if I fail again, Hitu? I really want to pass this time. I am just tired of trying."

Hitesh was helping Preeti with her studies for her final semester exams. It was one in the morning when Preeti finally put her book aside in exhaustion and rested her head on her brother's shoulders.

"If you fail, you try again."

◆

23/6/2007

All my classmates from computer engineering are preparing for their placements. I don't need to since I have not cleared my exams. I should be immune to this by now. This sinking feeling that comes over me every time I fail. I have failed so many times that I have lost count. I have humiliated myself so often that failure should no longer feel like a new experience. But somehow it does. It hurts every single time. And it hurts a little more. I feel as if I sink a little more each time, lose another chunk of me... I am afraid that by the end of it all, I will be left with nothing.

◆

23/9/2007

Oh my god! I cleared the exam! I can't believe I passed! I am a computer engineer. Oh my god! This can't be real. I want to go to the roof of the highest building and shout in joy, announce to the world that I did it! I did it despite being a dumb nut. I made it! This success belongs more to Hitu than it does to me. I feel so blessed today. I know I have made everyone proud. I wanted to tell mama and papa in person, but I just could not hold back the excitement and ended up telling them over the phone. I feel like I am going to explode!

◆

8/10/2007

Yesterday was the best day of my otherwise dull life. I felt happy. I was so happy that I couldn't even write in the diary even though I wanted to. I missed my convocation but mama and papa made it up for me... I will never forget what they did for me. I will never forget the look of pride and happiness on their faces.

◆

"Congratulations, Preeti!" Aarti exclaimed along with her husband, the nurse and the support staff, who had been working with them for so long that they were now considered family.

The room was decorated with balloons. A big banner read "Congratulations Chutki!"

Tears welled up in Preeti's eyes. A huge black forest cake rested on her father's bedside table.

"It's your convocation ceremony slash party," said Hitesh, grinning from ear to ear.

"You knew?" Preeti asked in amazement.

"We both did!" said nani, hugging Preeti tightly.

Preeti walked over to her father's bed. "Papa, are you proud of me?" she asked with tears in her eyes.

"Always been!" he said, tears running down his face.

"Preeti, we are all immensely proud of you!" added her mother.

"But I am yet to get placed, mama..." said Preeti thoughtfully.

"Don't worry about it, Preeti, we all know that you will get a fantastic job in a great company. It's only a matter of time," said her father reassuringly.

"I hope I get one quickly. It took me five years to complete my engineering. I am running out of time already."

"Preeti, look at me," said her mother, sitting next to her. "Stop beating yourself up, beta. You need to give yourself credit for what you've accomplished. There aren't too many people with learning disabilities who have conquered their demons as well as you have."

Preeti gave her a puzzled look.

"Preeti, do you remember Mr. Mehta, who collected your Math board exam paper after you wrote it at nani's place?"

"Hmm...."

"We were concerned about what you were going to do after your tenth exams. Your constant struggle with Math was not hidden from us. Although we tried to motivate you and thought it looked like a lack of focus and disinterest from your end, it was only after your board exams that I realized that the problem ran deeper. So I spoke to Mrs. Mehta who is a teacher. After I discussed with her the difficulties you faced in detail and let her take a look at your notebooks for different subjects over the years, she told me that in all likelihood, you have dyscalculia – a form of learning disability that affects a person's ability to understand numbers. Everything made sense then. You have always been so good in languages, but have suffered in subjects that involved calculations.

"You must be thinking why we never told you. We didn't because we thought it would have made you conscious; we didn't want you to think that you were lesser than others in some way. That was never the case anyway and never will be. You were and are just as capable, if not more, than any other person of your age. And for this very reason, I pushed you to pursue computer engineering. I knew it was going to be tough. But I also knew that you were tougher. We all did. I have always envisioned my little girl to be a strong, independent woman and I knew that if you could handle this challenge, you could handle anything. I knew that if you could overcome this handicap, no hurdle, no matter how big, would ever intimidate you again."

"I...I..." Preeti tried to speak through the lump in her throat. A sense of relief came over her. All those years of thinking that she was dumb and incompetent, the constant failures, there was a reason after all, and she had conquered that reason. For the first time in her life, she felt immensely proud of herself. She had risen above everything within her that was pulling her back. Tears of joy trickled down her cheeks as she buried her face in her mother's chest.

"You can conquer everything, Chutki," said her mother stroking her daughter's hair.

"Yes, I can, mama. Yes, I can."

◆

7/7/2008

I have appeared for fourteen interviews in the last six months... still nothing. This is getting embarrassing. I don't know what to say to the neighbours when they ask me if I've got a job. Last weekend mama suggested that perhaps papa could use his influence to help me get a job, I refused.

◆

9/11/2008

I did it! After seven months and seventeen interviews, I finally did it! It's a bittersweet moment. I finally have a job but I will have to move to Mumbai. How will I manage? I have never been on my own before. It's scary... and I won't be able to see mama and papa as frequently anymore. And Hitu too. I wonder if this job is worth being away from the people who mean everything to me.

◆

"Hitu, I don't want to take up that job."

"Hmmm... Chutki, I know you are scared. I felt the same way when I had to move to the hostel."

"But Hitu, at least you were in the same town! I won't be able to see mama and papa as often, and you and nani as well..."

"Fine, let's say you don't take this offer. Let's say you find a better job here. But what about tomorrow? A year later? Five years later? Are you never going to look for other opportunities? Are your choices always going to be determined by where our parents live? No, right? What will you do when you get married? Get your husband to live with us?"

"Shut up, Hitu. I don't want to get married..."

"That's just silly. You need to take chances. You need to move out of your comfort zone. You need to step outside and face the world."

"I don't know, Hitu..."

"Yes, you do, Chutki. It's time to grow up."

◆

10/8/2009

Hitu left yesterday after helping me settle down in the new apartment. Everything feels so strange. Everything about this city seems so different, so rushed. Even the air feels different.

I could barely sleep last night. It's so noisy with all the cars and impolite people. I feel terribly alone. This was a huge mistake. I'm already thinking about going back.

◆

13/11/2009

The last three months in office have been amazing! I couldn't have asked for a better workplace and colleagues. Everything happens for a reason. Papa's health has stabilized as well. Everyone is happy. And nani and Hitu are moving back to our house with mama and papa. I am so thrilled! I can't wait to go home during the long weekend break next month. I have also applied for additional leave. We are finally going to live together as a family under one roof!

◆

23/12/2009

I am finally home! I feel like I have travelled back in time. Nothing has changed. Even my bedroom is still the same: the same bed with the same Barbie bedcover! Mama has left everything untouched. The parrots are raiding the mango tree outside as I write this. They are making so much noise right now, just like they used to when I was a little girl. Every little thing that we do together gives me so much joy. I had forgotten what it feels like to sit down together as a family for breakfast. I don't know how I am going to leave this time. It's going to be harder than I imagine.

◆

24/12/2009

I spoke to mama some time back. She is still stuck on that topic. God! Why can't they understand that I am just not interested?

◆

"No, I don't like anyone from office! And no, I don't want you to look around for me."

"But beta, this is the right age to get married!" said Preeti's mother.

"Mama, please! I have told you countless times! I just don't..." Preeti choked. "I just don't feel comfortable around anyone else, and you know why, mama."

"Beta, I know what you've gone through as a little girl. I really feel guilty for not being there when you needed me, my child... but you need to understand that if one man has hurt you in the past, it does not mean that every man is going to hurt..."

"No, mama. You don't know... if you did, we wouldn't be having this discussion right now."

◆

1/1/2010

Oh my god! What a fantastic start to the New Year! Hitu gave me such a wonderful surprise!

◆

Hitesh sat on the lawn in their garden while Preeti swayed on the swing under the shade of the mango tree, sunlight struggling to filter through the dense canopy of the leaves.

"Hmm... Chutki, I have to tell you something."

"Yes, Hitu."

"Ermm... I am seeing someone."

"What!" she yelled in surprise, getting off the swing to sit next to her brother. "Are you really seeing someone? No way!"

"Shh... promise me, you won't tell anyone. Promise?"

"Who is she? Where did you meet her? Since when have you been dating her? Tell me, tell me everything!" she exclaimed.

"First, promise me that you won't tell anyone."

"Yeah, yeah, I won't. Now tell me," she said impatiently.

"Her name is Varsha. I met her in office. I've been seeing her for a month and…"

"A month! Hitu, a month! And you're telling me now! What the hell! Just wait, I'm going to tell everyone now," she said, standing up hastily.

Hitesh pulled her back down by her hand.

"I didn't want to tell you over the phone, Chutki. I was waiting for you to come here so that I could tell you in person."

"Don't make lame excuses. And let go of my hand," she said gruffly.

"Sorry, Chutki! I really didn't want to tell you about her over the phone."

"Fine," she said, curling her lips in mock disdain. Moments later, her face lit up and she smiled. "Tell me about her, Hitu. What does she look like? Do you have a photo of her?" she said and laughed as she looked at her brother's confused expression.

"I've been waiting for her all this time, Chutki," he said dreamily.

"Oh my god! Let me hear you say that again!"

◆

5/4/2010

I bought a car! One new year resolution done!

◆

17/7/2010

Hitu is getting married! I am so excited! Everyone loves Varsha. She is such a sweetheart! The priest has given us a date for the wedding: 12th of December. Just four months to go! I don't want to go back to Mumbai. How will I focus on work when I will be daydreaming about Hitu riding a ghodi while we all dance in the baraat?

◆

9/8/2010

I have my heart set on the apartment I saw today. I'm definitely buying it. I am going to have my own place!

This has been such a great year... Back in school and even in college I never imagined I would ever achieve such milestones in life. And yet, slowly but surely, it's all happening. Sometimes it feels so surreal. Sometimes I feel scared that all this will come to an end.

◆

"Hitu!" Preeti yelled.

Her brother came running into the kitchen, his phone jammed to his ear, looking visibly flustered. Preeti snatched it and ended the call, coating it with flour.

"Preeti! Why the hell did you do that? I was speaking to the band—"

"Hitu, calm down."

"Preeti, they just cancelled and we have four days to go. Where will I find another band in—"

"Hitu, calm down!" Preeti yelled at him this time. "You've been shouting and arguing with people all morning. It's your wedding! I want you to be happy and not so stressed out!"

"Seriously, Hitesh bhaiya, you need to chill out," said Vanshika, their fifteen-year-old cousin who was helping Preeti in the kitchen.

"Hmm..." said Hitesh absentmindedly.

"I know it's chaotic and overwhelming, but you don't need to handle everything. Arjun mamaji is here, Ashwin kaka... everyone is here," said Preeti.

"Hmm," said Hitesh.

"Oh come on! Cheer up!" Preeti poked him in the ribs. Hitesh smiled weakly. "Everything is going to be fine, Hitu," she said and hugged her brother.

◆

2/12/2010

Two days to go! It feels like a carnival is going on in our house!

◆

"Where is Hitu, mama?" asked Preeti.

"He just left to get some pooja material. Why, beta?"

"Ashwin kaka was calling Hitu. He wanted the keys of the scooter," said Preeti.

"Beta, tell kakaji that Hitesh has taken the scooter."

"Okay."

Preeti had barely stepped on the stairway to go upstairs when the landline phone started ringing. Preeti rushed back to get it.

"Hello?"

"Hello madam, do you have a white Scooty with the number GJ13AC1129?"

"Yes, who is this?"

"Madam, I'm sorry to tell you this, but there has been an accident..."

Hitesh's body lay in the middle of the living room wrapped in a white shroud. His face lay exposed; swollen and drained of colour, he was beyond recognition. The smoke from incense sticks eddied hypnotically. Their fragrance failed to camouflage the stench of death that lingered in the room. All the decorations in and around the house had been brought down. The orange marigolds that had been bought to deck up the house for Hitesh's wedding now lay solemnly over his lifeless form.

Preeti stood away from everyone else, barely breathing, unable to believe that her brother had passed away. She looked on at the proceedings with a glazed expression, not registering anything around her. The voices seemed to be coming from another world.

"Aarti, it's time…" said Preeti's uncle Divesh, holding her arms and trying gently to pull her away.

"No!" she screamed and threw her arms over her son's body protectively. "No one is taking my son away from me!"

Other family members joined in, trying to comfort her and coax her to step away, but she refused.

"No one is taking my son away from me," Aarti screamed, convulsing like a possessed woman.

"We have to take him..."

"Please," Pulkit cried, his hands joined together, "...please!"

"God! Why did you do this to us?" Aarti yelled.

Pulkit got off his wheelchair again with a loud thud, landing on his knees next to his son. He held Hitesh's face in his hands and said, "Why did you leave us like this?"

Aarti turned around and buried her face in Pulkit's chest, her sobs now muffled.

Preeti sat down, her legs unable to carry the weight of her grief, and watched in silence as her parents, helpless and shattered, wept like children. She couldn't get herself to go near Hitesh's body. The distance made it look like it was a dream. She watched him being taken away, her senses refusing to acknowledge that her beloved brother, her support system had left her forever.

◆

Preeti was in her new apartment, painting in a manic, trance-like state, oblivious to everything around her. Ever since she had returned to Mumbai two weeks ago, after spending close to a month in Baroda overseeing all the ceremonies and rituals following her brother's death, she didn't do anything other than paint.

The sound of the crackling fire as it consumed her brother's body haunted her every moment, making it impossible for her to function. Away from her parents and home, the truth of her brother's demise finally sunk its teeth into her skin, and the pain that she had bottled up inside her broke free. Her insides churned at the very thought of the gruesome tragedy that had wrecked their lives.

Tired of spending sleepless nights and drained by grief, she picked up her old box of colours one evening and started painting.

When she started off on the first empty canvas, she didn't know what she was going to paint; she just let her paintbrushes glide, and they religiously followed the trajectory of her angst. The choice of colours and strokes were all a reflection of what was going through her mind. The reds were the embers within her that refused to die. The blues were the rare instances when she was spent by her grief. The blacks were her moments of absolute weakness, the colour of the bottomless pit she had plunged into, falling through and through.

The colours spoke to her in whispers, narrating their own tale while she poured out her own. They allowed her to channel her life through them. They listened. They cared. They laughed. They cried. They reassured her that there was life waiting ahead, urging her forward with eager arms. And Preeti rushed to them with brush in hand.

Preeti has spent hours looking at her childhood photographs and reading her journals, looking for solace in memories of her brother. But despite realizing that time doesn't rewind, it only heals, she finds herself incapable of letting go. Preeti walks over to the window, draws the curtain aside and pulls the window open. A cool breeze hits her face and sets free a few strands of curly hair that fall over her eyes. She pulls herself up to settle on the narrow ledge and looks outside. The view is scintillating: lights from apartments and cars appear like a giant colony of fireflies against the velvet, ink-blue sky. The city surges forward, oblivious to the avalanche inside her. She shuts her eyes and breathes deeply, letting the air enter her lungs, feeling it make its way down her parched throat. And then she hears him.

"Chutki, come here!" he says.

She sees him now. He is standing downstairs, holding on to the rusty lamppost that rises up from the pavement. He is not looking at her, though; he has with him a little girl of ten with a bar of chocolate in her hand.

"Chutki, here, I know you like this. Now come, we have to go..."

It's strange that she can hear him from such a height. But she hears him all right, just like he is standing next to her, calling out to her in that sweet voice that defined her childhood.

Preeti's breathing picks up pace, the hair at the back of her neck rising in alarm. A current jolts through her body and she breaks into a cold sweat. She hears him again. Preeti covers her ears with her hands and shuts her eyes, refusing to look down.

"Please, don't!" she begs no one in particular and pushes her palms further against her ears until she can't hear anything but the blood rushing through her veins and her palpitating heart.

"Chutki, I'm waiting..."

Preeti exhales loudly. She opens her eyes to look down at where he was. It's a long way off. She fixates on the ground with a glazed expression, her mind in a state of turmoil. She takes a small step forward. Her entire life flashes before her eyes. *Papa's accident... Hitu cajoling her... Hitu handing out chocolates... Hitu praising her dance...Hitu making those pinky promises... Hitu teaching her Maths... Hitu calming her down... Hitu roughing up bullies... Hitu taking her for movies... Hitu telling her about his love life... Hitu excited... Hitu leaving the house... Hitu dead...dead...dead!*

Ding dong!

Preeti ignores the doorbell. It rings again. And again. Preeti stays frozen in her place, lost in her thoughts, wondering how soon it would be over if she leapt. The doorbell continues to ring, and suddenly her phone starts vibrating as well.

Buzzzz! Brrrrr! Buzzzzz! Brrrrrr!

Preeti turns around, knowing that it most probably is her mother calling her. Sure enough, the illuminated screen reads 'Mama calling...'

Preeti sighs and gets down to pick up her cellphone. The doorbell rings again. "Bloody asshole!" she murmurs under her breath.

"Hello mama, let me get back to you, I have something urgent to attend to," she says and disconnects the call.

Ding dong! Ding dong! Ding dong!

"I am coming!" Preeti screams in fury and rushes through the hallway into the living room. Without bothering to look through the peephole and half prepared to tear down the person, whoever it may be, Preeti swings the door open.

"Hi! Do you have some coffee I could use?"

She eyes the man standing outside her door for several seconds, partly amused but mostly suspicious. He is wearing a ridiculous green Afrowig and a bright pink shirt.

"Hi," she says with a poker face.

"I'm Sameer, your neighbour," he extends a hand through the metal gate.

She continues to look at him suspiciously, refusing to accept his hand.

"Ah...umm, so, do you have some coffee?"

"No, I don't," she says coldly.

She has never seen him before.

"Which flat is yours?" she asks, gesturing towards the five other flats on the floor, her hand firmly on the closed metal gate.

"That one," he says, pointing at a locked door without turning around.

"Do you always lock your door before going over to a neighbour's to ask for something?" she asks sarcastically.

"Huh?" he shoots a questioning look and turns around. "Oops!" He grins and points to the next apartment. "I just moved in this week..."

"Of course you have... Help! Help! Someone help!" Preeti suddenly screams with all her might.

"What? Hey... Huh... What did I do? Stop shouting!"

"Help! Help me! Thief! Thief!" Preeti screams, ignoring Sameer's questioning looks.

"What's wrong? What happened?" asks one of the neighbours, storming out of his house with his wife in tow.

"What's this commotion?" thunders another neighbour–an elderly man with an imposing built.

As the men flank Sameer, Preeti opens the metal gate and steps outside. "Uncle,this guy came here asking for some coffee and he claims to live here, but I have never seen him before. He first pointed to that flat," she gestures at the locked door, "and then that one. And look at the way he's dressed," she says contemptuously, wrinkling her nose. "I think the coffee was just a pretext to enter my house and rob me. I mean, just look at him... who dresses like this? It looks like a disguise, that too, a really bad one. And he is drunk as well."

"No, no, there's a party in my apartment, that's why I am dressed like..." Sameer starts to explain.

"You scoundrel," the old man barks and grabs Sameer by the collar of his shirt. "I know your kind very well. Just today in the newspaper I read about a theft in Worli. Two men came to an apartment, claiming to service home appliances, and robbed the residents."

"Oh yes!" the other neighbour exclaims and nods his head, "we read it too... I think one of them wore a wig just like that!"

"You are all getting it wrong," says Sameer. "I moved in just yesterday so you might not have seen me before. Please listen to me. You can come over to my apartment and see for yourself. We are having a party. You can ask any of my guests..."

"Uncle," says Preeti looking at the old man. "These are all lies. We should call the police and hand this man over to them. He is just trying to waste our time," she says angrily.

"Yes, yes, I agree," says the other neighbour's wife.

"At least come over to the apartment, it's only going to take a few minutes. If I am lying, then you can do whatever you want to," says Sameer.

"Even thieves these days speak such good English," the neighbour's wife mutters under her breath.

"He is right. There is no harm done," says the husband.

"Hmm," agrees the old man and lets go of Sameer's collar.

Sameer walks confidently to the apartment with the neighbours and Preeti trailing him. Turning the handle, he pushes the door, but it doesn't budge. He tries several times, but the door doesn't open.

He turns around and says, "These automatic locks… I still haven't gotten the hang of using them."

"I am calling the police now," says Preeti and pulls out her phone from her pyjama pocket.

"Please wait," says Sameer.

"What for?" growls the old man.

"Let me ring the bell, one of my guests will get the door. Please," he begs.

"Go on.That house has been shut for two years," says the old man, folding his arms.

Sameer rings the doorbell several times, but there is no response. "Akshay! Tara! Gurav! Nivi!" he yells, banging his fist on the door.

"There is no one in there. We can't hear anyone!" says the neighbour's wife.

"Actually, we all had a bit too much to drink. They may have passed out…" says Sameer.

"Do you have any more stories to tell or are we done here?" asks the old man.

"Let's just call the police now," says Preeti impatiently.

"Before we call the police, let's first talk to the watchman. I want to know how he let this man enter our society premises without any identification," says the old man.

The watchman arrives a little later.

"Do you know him?" asks the old man.

Ravi looks at Sameer curiously and says breathlessly, "No, I, I do not know this clown."

"You're going to jail..." Preeti screams at Sameer.

"Wait... wait!" he says.

Sameer removes his wig and swiftly combs his hair with his fingers. "Arrey! It's me..."

"Oh! Sameer saab!" says the watchman and salutes him.

Preeti's jaw drops in surprise.

The watchman continues, "I know Sameer saab. He moved here this week."

"Are you sure?" Preeti asks him.

"Yes madam. I don't forget. He give me *baksheesh* when I brought up his bags," he says and grins. "But what is problem, madam? Why you scream?"

"I... I am... nothing... you can leave," says Preeti, her voice barely a whisper.

The old man apologizes to Sameer and goes back to his apartment, as do the couple, casting irritated glances at Preeti.

"I am so, so sorry!" Preeti apologizes with loosely folded hands.

"It's okay," says Sameer. "I would probably have thought the same if I was in your place."

"I'm extremely sorry. I was just scared and I had not seen you before, so I thought that..."

"It's all right, really!" says Sameer and smiles. "Man, you have severe trust issues!"

"Oh no, I feel terrible, let me make it up to you... I could start with giving you some coffee," she says and smiles before walking towards her apartment.

Sameer smirks and follows her. "So, have you also moved here recently?" asks Sameer as Preeti opens the door to her apartment.

"About a month back and I don't go out much, so..."

"Hmm..." he says as he steps inside the apartment. "You haven't had much time to unpack..." he remarks casually, looking at the three brown cartons lying in one corner of the bare living room.

"Yes... been a little busy..."she says thoughtfully. "I will be back in a minute," she says walking into the kitchen.

Sameer walks around the living room and then flops into a bright orange beanbag. He can hear Preeti opening and closing kitchen cabinets.

"Don't you think it's kind of weird that I am sitting in your house right now and I don't even know your name?" he asks aloud while Preeti turns the kitchen upside-down.

She laughs and replies from the kitchen, "I am Preeti Thaker."

"And I am Sameer Arora, your friendly neighbourhood *thief*," Sameer says.

Preeti laughs aloud and continues to open jars, most of which are either empty or have coffee labels on them but contain some other condiment instead.

"I'm sorry I'm taking so much time..." Preeti apologizes.

"That's perfectly all right. I'm in no rush," he says and turns around casually to catch a glimpse of Preeti's bedroom. He can see paintings stacked on the floor haphazardly. He is taken aback by their number. Captivated, he moves forward, taking them in with eyes that refuse to settle on one canvas, thrilled by the colours that tell so many tales in such few strokes. His eyes come to rest on a canvas in the corner.

The painting depicts a haunting landscape of a forest: creepers and low-hanging branches silhouetted against an eerie blue light that breaks through the canopy of leaves overhead and falls like spotlights on the ground in no fixed pattern. A spectral figure stands under one such spotlight, its back to the viewer, quietly observing its surreal surroundings. The figure faces a circle of infinity whose lines keep merging into each other, the radius emitting a glow like the sun's. Yet it is not the sun. It is something else. Sameer continues to stare intently at the centre of the circle of infinity, squinting his eyes and trying to decipher the thought behind it when he hears the sound of glass breaking in the kitchen.

"Eew!" Preeti screams. "Shit!"

Sameer snaps out of his daze and rushes into the kitchen. "Is everything all ri—" he stops abruptly and freezes in his place. The kitchen floor is strewn with broken glass pieces and coffee.

"Are you all right?" he asks.

"Yeah…there was a huge cockroach and I dropped the jar," she says sheepishly and picks up a broom lying under the kitchen sink.

"This is turning out to be quite an eventful night for you," Sameer says.

"You have no idea!" she says and guffaws. "And I won't be able to give you any coffee. I'm sorry."

"That's all right. Have you had dinner yet?" he asks, looking at the scant kitchen counter, already knowing the answer.

"No…"

"Why don't you come over to my apartment? We can have dinner there."

"Thanks, but I think I'll pass."

"Oh come on! You can clean this mess later... we have pizza!"

"I have a few things to take care of..."

"That's a lame excuse. It's Friday night. Come on now!"

"It's okay, I can manage..."

"Oh, man! Aren't you a draamebaaz? Don't worry, I won't rob you."

Preeti laughs and nods her head. Although reluctant, she is disarmed by Sameer's genial nature and gives in to his request.

Ding dong! Ding dong!

Standing outside Sameer's apartment, Preeti can hear a phone ring from within the flat as Sameer dials a friend's number while his thumb presses firmly against the doorbell. After ten minutes of ringing the doorbell and calling non-stop, Sameer and Preeti hear the lock click. A pudgy man with chubby cheeks, a bushy beard and bloodshot eyes opens the door.

"Haraami!" he curses Sameer, takes a few steps towards a wine-coloured couch lying adjacent to the doorway, and plops down on it. Its occupant, a tall, slender girl, groans and shifts just enough to accommodate him. She murmurs incoherently and places her dupatta over her face before dozing off. The small circular table in front of the couch is crowded with beer bottles and unopened pizza boxes. Only one box lies open on the table, its contents emptied. A pretty, voluptuous girl snores noisily on the floor, her head resting on the couch behind her.

Sameer has been looking at Preeti with an amused expression while she takes in the scene. "That's Gurav," he whispers, pointing at the guy who opened the door for them. "And that's Nivi," he says pointing at the girl lying next to Gurav. "That's Tara," he says gesturing towards the other girl. "And..." he trails off while looking around the room.

"Wyaaccccck......ullllllll!" They hear someone throwing up.

"That would be Akshay," says Sameer and bursts out laughing. "Poor guy, he can't tolerate even a bit of liquor..."

Preeti smiles awkwardly, feeling out of place and regretting her decision to come to his apartment.

"Please make yourself comfortable," Sameer tells Preeti, gesturing towards the small dining table at the other end of the room. "I will be back in a minute. I need to check on Akshay, our delicate darling!"

Preeti pulls a chair for herself and settles down uneasily. The only two sounds in the apartment are that of Akshay vomiting in the bathroom and Tara snoring. Preeti fidgets with the keys to her apartment while she takes in the sights.

In one corner of the room, right next to the couch on which Gurav and Nivi lie, a few bulb-shaped lamps are suspended from the ceiling. Barring one wall, which is occupied with framed vinyl records and pop-art pieces, all the walls are painted a pristine white and stand bare. The music and art fan that she is, Preeti makes a subconscious mental note of it.

The events of the evening seem like a blur, almost like they are happening to another person at another time. Knowing herself, she can't believe she's sitting in a stranger's house at this time of the night with his drunken friends for company. But something about Sameer exudes safety. And moreover, she realizes that if it wasn't for him, then a government ambulance would have been picking up the pieces of her body strewn over the pavement at this time.

"I'm so sorry, I kept you waiting for so long," Sameer declares loudly, walking into the living room, slipping on a t-shirt, giving Preeti a brief glimpse of his torso. Preeti looks away, her eyes landing on Sameer's friends, and then puts her fingers to her lips looking back at him. Sameer exhales dramatically and grins. He tiptoes as he heads towards the table to pick up pizza boxes and a couple of Coke bottles and then walks back to Preeti. He places the pizza boxes on the table and sits down next to her.

"Phew!" he exhales. "I had to change because Akshay threw up on me," he says pointing at his t-shirt. "The price one pays for throwing a party," he murmurs.

Unsure of what to say, Preeti simply smiles. On the one hand she wants to leave, but on the other, she feels obliged to play along.

"Chicken Tikka…" Sameer reads aloud the handwritten note on one of the pizza boxes before opening it. "Let's start with that, shall we?"

"Sure."

"So… what do you do for a living?" he asks Preeti as he pours Coke into two glasses and opens the pizza box.

Preeti's stomach rumbles violently as she takes in the aroma of cheese and grilled chicken nuggets spread on the pizza. "I'm a manager in Obsoft. It's a software company in Malad," she says distractedly, her eyes on the pizza.

"Nice!" says Sameer extending the box to her, urging her to take a slice.

Preeti readily grabs a pizza slice and digs right into it. They spend the next two minutes in absolute silence, engrossed in eating, submitting to gluttony. Preeti is about to pick up another slice when the sound of vomiting fills the room.

She gags and covers her mouth while Sameer, sitting next to her, continues to relish the pizza as if he hasn't heard anything at all.

"I am sorry!" she apologizes. "Shouldn't you check on your friend again?"

"I will in some time. He's going to be fine. Trust me…" he says nonchalantly, taking another slice of pizza and handing it to Preeti. She smiles politely and takes it hesitantly, no longer in a mood to eat, her hunger pangs killed by the sound of Akshay vomiting.

When the silence becomes uncomfortable, Preeti feels compelled to ask Sameer a similar question about his occupation. "So, umm, what do you do?"

"I thought you would never ask," he smirks. "I deal with real estate. But it's nowhere near as interesting as the work you do, I am sure."

"A businessman, interesting. I wish the IT industry was half as appealing as it sounds," says Preeti, rolling her eyes.

"The grass is always greener on the other side..."

"I guess..."

"Have you moved to Mumbai recently?" Sameer asks.

"No, I have been here for quite some time... seven years actually. I moved into this apartment recently. What about you?"

"Same story, except that I have been in Mumbai for five years."

"I see," says Preeti.

"You must have a very hectic schedule. All folks in IT do, even Nivi. She is always cribbing about her work hours," he says, pointing to the girl lying fast asleep on the couch.

"Oh! Which company is she in?"

"Dano...Danev...Damer..."

"Danek Solutions?" suggests Preeti.

"Yeah, that's the one."

"Hmm..." Preeti trails off, her focus now on the last slice of pizza in the box.

"How do you manage to find time to paint?"

Preeti's eyes widen. "How do you know I paint?" she asks.

"While I was in your apartment waiting for you to get coffee, I could see your room and the paintings stacked against the wall."

"Okay," she says curtly. What she actually wants to do is scream and lunge at Sameer for violating her privacy, for peeking into a world she only shares with her memories.

"As you can see," says Sameer, pointing at the wall covered with popart frames, "I take a great interest in art, so I couldn't take my eyes off your brilliant work. Your brush strokes are absolutely exquisite as are your dramatic use of colours... but the most amazing thing about your paintings is that they hold a piece of you and they have a story to tell..."

"Did you see them up close?" she asks, her ears getting hot and her blood pumping.

"No, I saw what I saw from the living room. In fact, I could only see one of your works clearly – the one of a shadow-like figure in a forest staring at a circle. The rest I saw vaguely, but that was enough to capture their essence," he says smiling and opens another pizza box.

"Hmm, the circle of life and death," whispers Preeti, looking away.

"Death?" Sameer looks puzzled.

"I should leave now," Preeti says abruptly and gets up.

Sameer gets up from his chair, understanding that Preeti is upset about something.

"Umm, did I offend you about something? I hope not..."

"No."

"Does it have something to do with the fact that I saw your paintings?"

"No, no."

From her flushed appearance Sameer can tell she is lying. "I'm extremely sorry that I looked in the direction of your bedroom. It was a horrible, horrible thing to do. I should have looked elsewhere."

Preeti looks at him incredulously for a moment and then bursts out laughing, realizing how foolishly she has reacted. "I am so sorry, I just… it's not your fault, of course not."

"Next on the menu, Paneer pizza then," he declares.

Preeti smiles and settles back in her chair. "I am so embarrassed."

"It's okay…"

"I have not been in a good frame of mind, and this has been such a strange evening…" she tries to justify her behaviour.

"Did you just go through a break-up?"

She smiles and shakes her head.

"Then who is it that you are looking for in your paintings?" he says, looking right into her eyes.

Preeti is stunned into silence for a moment. Her eyes well up and she looks down, not wanting to show her raw emotions to a person she barely knows. Sameer sits in silence, patiently waiting for her to open up. He hands her a glass of water. "This time I did intrude, didn't I? I'm sorry," he says softly.

Preeti wipes her eyes, looks up at him through her tears and says, "No, it's okay. You are right. I am looking for someone in my paintings, trying to find closure for something that shouldn't have happened, trying to reason the unreasonable…"

Sameer is listening to her in rapt attention, not breaking eye contact and trying to soothe her without saying a word, reaching out to her by just being there and listening to her. Preeti finds herself unable to hold back the avalanche of emotions within her and continues to talk, going against her own nature.

"Have you ever lost someone close to you? Someone who's at the core of your universe, the hero of all your stories… when that happens, it isn't just the loss of one life, it's the loss of two lives – one who found another world, perhaps… and one who is left behind…" Preeti pauses and takes a deep breath, failing to understand what has taken over her and why she has revealed her pain to a stranger.

"Oh..." For a moment, Sameer's body seems to dull, but he regains his composure the very next moment.

"I'm searching for my brother in my paintings. Maybe he has moved to some realm beyond this space and time, maybe I will find the answers through my paintings... I don't know..." she trails off to wipe her tears and then looks at Sameer. "You must think I am crazy. We've only met a couple of hours ago, had the most ridiculous misunderstanding in our first meeting, and now I am sitting in your apartment talking to you about something that does not make any sense... you must be thinking I am crazy."

"No, I don't think you are crazy," he says in a pacifying tone.

"... and I am talking about dead people and finding them in my paintings..." she continues to blabber as if she hasn't heard him.

"Preeti, you are not crazy," he says looking right at her and squeezing her shoulder gently.

Sameer's empathy encourages her to pour her heart out, the burden on her shoulders lifting finally after weeks of struggle.

"... when the door to the incinerator opened and they slid his body inside, I finally accepted that he was not going to wake up or come back. Until that point, I kept convincing myself that he would wake up, something would happen, some miracle... even now, on some days, I wake up thinking he will come back into our lives and everything will be fine."

"I am so sorry," says Sameer despite knowing that his condolences would mean nothing to her grieving heart.

"I must sound so dumb right now..." Preeti snivels.

"No, you don't. It's okay to feel that hollowness within you. And it's okay to be in denial. They are all stages of grief."

"How do you know?"

"Trust me... I do!"

"I don't understand what the problem is! It's not being used anyway, and the owner of the apartment doesn't even stay here," says Preeti, throwing her hands up in the air.

"Madam, two days back also you made so much noise, calling Sameer saab thief and robber. You make problems always," says the watchman Ravi, tapping his laathi on the ground.

"That was a misunderstanding and it was resolved between your saab and me. "But please try to understand. Since I don't have a parking space, I park my car outside the society premises, and every time, those stupid children from the slum come and either puncture my car tyres or steal stuff from the car. They broke the window and stole the music system once... and today, they have written all kinds of dirty words on the window panes of my car... those slum dwellers should be thrown out from there and their dumb children should be thrashed."

"Madam... I... stay... in that slum," the guard says with clenched fists.

"Oh! I meant, I... I mean, everyone is not bad, just some of them, only some of them are bad and they should be thrown out," Preeti says in an effort to make amends. Ravi starts walking away without saying anything.

"Ravi bhaiyya!" shouts Preeti.

"I not your bhaiyya, madam. And don't park your car there, I tell you last time. I leave now, I have work," he shouts.

The guard continues to walk away from Preeti. She loses her cool and yells, "Oye, watchman! Don't try to act too smart. I am going to park my car here, you do whatever you feel like doing."

The guard turns around and yells back, "I will puncture the tyres of your car myself."

"You rascal! You won't dare! I'm going to have you thrown out of this society."

On hearing this, the watchman furiously walks towards Preeti. A car pulls into the parking space right next to the spot where Preeti is standing. Sameer steps out of the car and greets her.

"Hi! How are you?"

"I am fine, thanks. How are you?"

"Oh madam!" says Ravi angrily.

Sameer turns around to face Ravi.

"Saab!" says Ravi as he salutes Sameer, his voice suddenly mellow.

"What happened?" asks Sameer, judging from the watchman's previously angry tone that something is amiss.

"Madam wants to park car here, this parking belongs Poonawala saab. I tell her no. *Ulta* she tell me that I live in stupid slum and everyone is thief there. Like she told you that day. This madam is mad, she think everyone is thief," he says angrily.

"No, that's not how it all went down..." Preeti starts explaining.

"You didn't get a parking slot when you bought the flat?" Sameer looks puzzled.

"Err... wanted to save up so had told the broker to negotiate on my behalf. Never checked on the parking and so far, had been managing..." Preeti tries to explain.

"Say no more. We'll figure it out," Sameer assures.

Sameer talks to Ravi and finds a middle ground by letting Preeti park in his parking space.

"That's very generous of you, but I can't. You will have to park outside the society and then you will have the same problems I've been facing," says Preeti.

"Not at all. I own two parking spaces here and my other car is still in my hometown. I don't think my younger brother has any intention of letting it go anytime soon," says Sameer with a grin.

"But we need to sign papers first and do the settlement..."

"What papers? What settlement?" he asks.

"I'm going to buy that additional parking space from you. We will obviously need to sign some documents," she says.

"But I'm not selling it to you!"

"But I can't..."

"Yes, you can. It's no big deal. Unless of course you want to still park your car outside and one fine day, not find it there. That would also solve the problem, wouldn't it?"

Preeti sighs.

◆

"Hey!"

"Hi! Please come in. What's up? Don't ask me for coffee, because I don't have any," says Preeti, letting Sameer into her apartment.

"Nah! It's your lucky day! Today I have some coffee for you," he grins and raises the transparent coffee pot in his hand, the liquid inside it making waves like turbulent seawaters. "And don't forget the cookies, my famous burnt almond cookies," he adds,gently shaking the tin box in his other hand.

"Did you bake them yourself?"

"Yes."

"Seriously?"

"Yes."

Although Preeti had candidly spoken about her brother's demise and how it affected her on the day she first met Sameer, in hindsight she felt somewhat embarrassed for having let her guard down so easily. She made a resolution that it wouldn't happen again. But Sameer's geniality seemed to break through her defences on every occasion. The way he smiled, warm and inviting, one couldn't help but lay their trust in his palms. As they settled down on the beanbags, coffee mugs in hands and munching on cookies, she couldn't fathom why a man she barely knew would go out of his way to make her feel so comfortable.

"The cookies are divine! You need to share the recipe with me. In fact, you need to teach me how to bake, I have never tried my hand at it."

"Just drop by sometime, we will bake together. I find cooking and baking rather therapeutic."

"I can't cook if my life depended on it," she says. "I burnt Maggi once."

Sameer burst out laughing. "Oh come on! You've got to be exaggerating..."

"I am not, seriously."

"Then how do you manage? You've been on your own all this while..."

"I can just make daal and chawal... sometimes rajma. I usually get the sabzi from a nearby restaurant."

"Well, looks like your prayers have been answered. You can now get sabzi from your friendly neighbour who cooks brilliantly and is not a thief!"

Preeti bursts out laughing.

"My name is Sameer and I'm not a thief," he says, with glazed eyes and an expressionless face, mimicking a certain Bollywood actor.

Preeti laughs even harder, turning beetroot red in the process.

"What else? How was your day? How was office?" Sameer asks.

"Umm, yeah okay," says Preeti.

She had not started going to office after returning from Baroda. She had woken up late in the morning and spent the afternoon painting. Sameer knew that she had not gone to work that day. He had noticed her car while parking his own, covered in a thick film of dust.

"It's a good thing you've resumed work. Very often, people fall into this trap while grieving, bringing their lives to a halt, not realizing that it only magnifies their pain."

"Actually, I didn't go to office today," she says after a moment's silence.

"I can understand why not..."

"I just don't feel like it, you know. Not just office, but everything... everything seems so unimportant. I have fallen deep into the trap, haven't I?"

"But the important thing is that you realize that you have, that's the first stage of recovery. Don't think too much. Start going to office, trust me, it will feel good."

"It's difficult..."

"I know it is, but remember, the world doesn't stop for your grief. I know you are stronger than you think. You can keep pace with the world. Even outrun it, if you want to!"

"Hmm... thank you, Sameer," she says taking the last sip of her coffee.

◆

"Hi everyone!" says Preeti, feeling conscious as she steps into Sameer's apartment. Akshay, Tara, Gurav and Nivi are parked on the couch. Sameer has invited Preeti over for an impromptu party at his apartment. It has been a little less than two weeks since Preeti met him.

"Guys, everyone!" Sameer announces loudly, "This is Preeti, my neighbour. She knows all of you very well." He bursts out laughing.

"Oh! So you are the one who almost got Sameer jailed," says Akshay.

"I didn't mean to..." starts Preeti, blushing fiercely.

"He is just taking your case, Preeti, relax! He is a big bully... except when he is drunk and puking in a toilet," says Sameer amid peals of laughter.

"Welcome to the gang, girl!" says Nivi handing her a beer bottle.

"Thanks!" says Preeti and settles down beside her.

"Chalo, let's continue the game, she is on our team," says Nivi putting her arm around Preeti.

Preeti's gaze falls on the Scrabble board on the table in front of them. She starts reading the words: bastard, asshole, jackass. She looks confused. Tara, who is in the other team and is sitting right opposite Preeti on the other side of the table, bursts out laughing. "Look at her face!"

"We play a modified version of Scrabble. You are only allowed to form cuss words or any dirty word. And don't look so shocked, we are only warming up... oh! I forgot to mention, you are also allowed to form cuss words in Hindi," says Nivi, grinning.

"It's our turn, right?" asks Gurav.

"Yeah, we made jackass, remember?" says Sameer,who's sitting right next to Preeti.

"C-H-U-T-I-Y-A," Tara says aloud as she arranges the letters on the board.

Preeti is surprised by her brazenness. A few minutes into the game, she starts feeling rather uncomfortable around them. She finds them strange and the game rather childish. But she sits in silence, listening to their jokes and occasionally smiling.

"You are allowed to talk, you know," Gurav tells Preeti.

"Arrey! She is planning her escape. She has been eyeing that door for several minutes now." Tara states her astute observation and guffaws.

Preeti laughs awkwardly, feeling embarrassed. "No, no, that's not why. I'm expecting a courier, you know," she lies.

"They have found a new *bakra* in you, Preeti, careful!" says Sameer. "You should do the honours now," he says, pushing the Scrabble letters' stand in her direction.

"Yes, yes, show us what you've got," says Akshay in mock enthusiasm.

"Chup, saale! Let her channel her inner Shakti Kapoor," says Gurav.

"Shut up, you all!" says Nivi.

D-U-M-B. Preeti forms the word on the board.

The rest of the gang bursts out laughing.

"Arrey! Junior KG gaalis not allowed. This is cheating!" yells Gurav.

"Miss Preeti, the nation wants to know why you've done this?" shouts Sameer, gesturing wildly and talking like a popular news channel anchor.

Preeti cracks up listening to their banter. She wonders if she has judged them too swiftly.

◆

The next day, Preeti reaches home after a long day at work, her first in office after the hiatus following her brother's death. She can feel the exhaustion chipping away at her bones. She throws her bag and her white floral scarf carelessly on the floor and flops onto a beanbag. She kicks away her black kitten heels and opens the top two buttons of her blue pinstriped shirt, exposing her white bra underneath. Stretching one leg on the beanbag placed in front of her, she crosses her other leg over it, bringing her foot to rest on her knee, and starts massaging the aching sole. Preeti closes her eyes and lets her mind go blank.

Preeti's cellphone buzzes. Preeti does not budge, not wanting to let anything come in the way of her and the nothingness that is holding her in a tight embrace.

Ping! Ping!

Preeti lets out a groan and mutters, "Shut up!"

Ping!

She exhales loudly and finally opens her eyes. "This better not be a stupid forwarded joke or something," she says angrily as she tries to grab her purse, which lies just beyond her reach. Preeti does not get up from the beanbag. Instead, she rolls over on it, and with her stomach resting on the seat, extends her hand out as far as she can in the direction of her handbag, the palm of her other hand resting on the floor to balance her. After struggling for several minutes, she ends up falling face first on the floor.

"Might as well have gotten up and picked up the bloody thing," she says angrily.

Not bothering to stand up, she simply props herself up on her elbows as she lies on the floor, caking the front of her shirt and trousers in a fine layer of dust. She fishes out her phone and swipes the screen. '4 messages from Sameer' – the WhatsApp notification reads.

Hey naybor!
Back frm ofc yet?
Wat plans 4 dinner?
I'm makn Matar Paneer. Want sum?
Preeti smiles and responds:

Hey!
Yeah, reachd home a few minutes bk.
Dinner, idk yet, will make something…
Thnx but I will pass.

Shut up n come ovr!

No, seriously, it's ok.

Let me tempt u.

Sameer sends her a picture of the dish he is cooking – bright green peas and chunks of cottage cheese simmering in a bright orange gravy, coriander leaves thrown on top, and a generous glob of butter melting away in the centre. Preeti is indeed tempted by the sight.

Looks fabulous!

IT IS! Now come ovr!

All right

Awesome! Should have told me before, itna naatak!

Preeti gets up from the floor and dusts her clothes. She freshens up quickly, ties her scraggly hair in a bun and makes her way to Sameer's house with a bottle of Coke.

"Hi!" Sameer flashes a broad grin as he opens the door. He is wearing a dark blue apron over a pair of grey shorts and a white T-shirt.

"Hey there!" says Preeti, handing over the Coke bottle.

"Oh my god! A brand new Coke bottle! I have always wanted one of these," says Sameer, cradling it lovingly in his arms.

Preeti bursts out laughing.

"I... oh god! I am so embarrassed right now. What was I thinking?" she says wiping a tear as Sameer closes the door behind her.

"I was joking, relax! On a serious note, matar paneer and Coke is my favourite combination," he says earnestly.

"Seriously?"

"I am still joking," says Sameer with a straight face.

Preeti slaps her forehead and follows Sameer into the kitchen. While he makes the chapattis, Preeti stands with her back against the refrigerator, watching him roll them out perfectly, feeling ashamed of her less-than-perfect cooking skills.

"So, how was your day?" he asks, turning sideways and meeting her eyes momentarily before shifting his gaze back to the burner.

"It was good. Tiring, but good. You were absolutely right. I should have resumed office earlier. I would have been a lot less miserable then."

"Never too late..."

"I didn't think about Hitu at all during the day, you know. I was just so caught up with everything. I wonder if he'll completely disappear from my conscious mind after a few more days once I am busy with work..."

"He won't disappear, that's for sure. He will come to you when you want him to: when you are happy, when you are sad, when something big happens in your life and you want to run to him and tell him before you tell anyone else, he will be there."

"I don't know… I feel guilty, I don't know how to explain this… I just, I feel horrible. I feel like I'm leaving him behind," says Preeti, her voice cracking.

"Perhaps he's thinking the same way right now. Wherever he is, he may be feeling bad that he left you behind," he says and turns off the burner. Wiping his hands on the apron, he continues, "You shouldn't feel bad or guilty about anything. You need to move ahead in life. You won't be insulting your brother's memories if you do." He takes a step forward and puts his hand on her shoulder, trying to console her as she weeps silently.

"Do you think he would want you to sit around, do nothing, and grieve over him for the rest of your life?" asks Sameer.

"No," mouths Preeti through the lump in her throat and breaks down.

Sameer draws her close to himself, letting her cry on his chest.

"Preeti, everyone is going to lose someone they love dearly. If they are unlucky, maybe more than one. If everyone were to give up on their lives, the world would be a very sad place to live in, no?"

"Hmm," says Preeti, emerging from the cocoon of Sameer's arms and wiping her tears.

"I think I know what will cheer you up right now – matar paneer and Coke served by your friendly neighbour who is not a thief!" he says and laughs.

◆

Preeti and Sameer are having lunch at Preeti's flat on a Saturday afternoon. It has become a part of their routine to meet up and have atleast one meal together during the day. Mostly it's dinner as both Preeti and Sameer are at work during the day, but on weekends, breakfast or lunch seems the perfect change.

It has barely been a little over a month since they first met, and Preeti already considers Sameer her closest friend. It surprises her tremendously how quickly he has become an indispensable part of her life and how effortlessly the story of her life leaves her lips in his presence. Those chapters of her life that she had tucked away under the surface of her skin, in her cells and her blood, they seem to have found their release.

"I used to wonder why every other kid in my class had a normal family and not me. I was very bitter. As I grew older, that sourness only grew on me. I felt like I had been cheated, that I had been robbed of everything that I deserved, of experiencing a father-daughter bond, or feeling the warmth of a mother-daughter relationship. I have spent countless hours trying to find a reason why I got less than most. And I just keep going round and round in circles. Have you ever felt that way? That you've been handed a raw deal?" asks Preeti.

"Well, we all do at some stage in life," says Sameer.

"I really wish I could turn back time and write my life over. Papa would have never had that horrible accident and all of us would have lived together. Everything would have been picture perfect. And Hitu would still be alive, of course. Life would be so different. I would be a different person. Mama tells me that everything happens for a reason and if I had not gone through all the experiences that I have, I would have never turned out to be half the person I am today. Honestly, I couldn't care less. I would much rather have been a weaker but happier person. I have paid too high a price."

"Why wish for something that will never be? That ends in nothing but heartbreak. We wish, then we think about how things would be if our wishes came true. And we feel happy thinking about those things. But then we wake up and realize that our wishes don't have wings. And it hurts because all the happiness that we thought of was never real. Hold on to what you have, try to find your happiness in what is, rather than what should or could have been," says Sameer.

"And what if one does not have anything at all? I wake up every morning thinking about papa, hoping and praying that he makes it through the day, and when night falls, I pray that the next morning when I wake up, he will be alive and well. Hitu's death came as a huge shock to both mama and papa. They are both devastated. If tomorrow something were to happen to papa..."

"Since we can't envision the future, why even attempt to? And if we must, why should we think of bad things? Life is beautiful. Let's stay positive... don't hold yourself back, Preeti. Why be a caterpillar when you have the wings to be a butterfly?" Sameer says, placing an arm on Preeti's knee.

"Hmm...," Preeti says, looking down at her plate and falling silent.

After finishing their meal, they stand near the window, looking at the traffic whizzing by, at the grey skies staring back at them.

"Sameer?"

"Uh-hmm?"

"I'm glad I have you."

"So am I, Preeti... so am I!" he says, putting an arm around her.

◆

"I wonder who's uglier, that chick or the ghost haunting her house..." Akshay ponders aloud as he waits for his turn to get inside the car while Gurav, Preeti and Nivi squeeze into the back seat of Sameer's silver Tata Indigo outside Alfred Cinema on Grant road. Bored of their soirées and karaoke nights, Tara had suggested that they watch a B-grade horror movie in a cheap theatre. It was a crazy idea, but one that appealed to all of them.

Preeti was not too keen, but was drawn into their madness, as she had been in the past.

"*Zabaan sambhaal*! You're talking about your bhabhi," says Gurav.

"*Tharki, saala...*" mutters Tara audibly.

"Let's go for a long drive guys, looks like it's going to rain. Should be fun," says Sameer, sticking his face out of the window and looking at the overcast skies.

"I am hungry, yaar!" says Nivi.

"Me too!" says Preeti.

"Nivi, you are such a hog! You single-handedly emptied half the popcorn bucket!" says Sameer.

"Seriously! I only got the salty leftovers," cribbed Akshay.

"We will go to McDonald's ka drive-in and get something, *chalega*?"

"Sounds good," everyone says in unison.

Sameer turns on the radio and everyone starts singing the popular Hindi song playing on it.

"We should come for another movie to this place," says Preeti all of a sudden.

Everyone stops singing and turns around to look at her.

"My my! Someone's developed a taste for dirty horror movies," says Nivi laughing.

"Aha! I always knew that there was a monster hiding behind that innocent face," says Gurav.

"Arrey, no, not like that..." Preeti tries to explain.

"Too late now, too late," says Tara.

"Shut up, you guys!" says Preeti and smiles.

Despite the bleak view outside, with raindrops hitting the windows as they zip past deserted roads and lone streetlights, Preeti feels a warmth spreading through her, a warmth she has not known before, the warmth of friendship. Sameer catches her eye and grins at her in the rearview mirror.

◆

"I used to be a real brat… and this rajma is freaking awesome!" says Sameer, stuffing his mouth with a spoonful of rajma chawal. Preeti has invited him over to her place for dinner on Monday night. He starts talking about his childhood after Preeti complains that he has never told her anything about himself.

"Thanks! It's one of those few things that I prepare well. It's my nani's recipe," says Preeti.

"So… we had this mansion because we lived in a joint family: my parents, my dada-dadi, my uncle, his wife and their three children. I was the youngest among four kids. And the leader of the gang. I used to come up with all sorts of schemes and make my cousins execute my plans while I sat back and watched the show," he says laughing aloud. "I remember this one time… I was like, chalo, let's paint uncle's car. Everyone thought it was a great idea."

"You've got to be kidding me!"

"Arrey, no! I'm serious. I was about seven and my oldest cousin was ten. So you can imagine… anyway, our house was getting painted at the time so we had these open cans of paint lying in the garage. My uncle and dad had gone to the office together in dad's car. All of us headed to the garage after telling our mothers that we were going to the playground. I remember giving everyone directions – 'Manju, paint that door properly, you left a spot.' By the time we had finished painting, my uncle's black Fiat had a white left side and a pink right side. We went back to the house. I told my cousins not to tell anyone. They asked me why not. I was like, it's going to be a surprise for uncle," says Sameer, laughing hysterically at this point.

"Oh my god! I can't imagine the look on your uncle's face!" says Preeti, howling.

"They found out of course – we couldn't take the paint off our hands – and the hiding that my cousins got, oh man! My parents were cool, though. I could see that dad was trying really hard not to laugh. I got away easily."

"You were seriously a brat!"

"I have so many childhood stories... my parents always bailed me out, no matter what I did. One time I was caught distributing porno magazines in school..."

"Really? How old were you at the time?"

"I was twelve," says Sameer thoughtfully.

"Oh my god! When I was twelve, my only concern in life was passing at math."

"I can tell," says Sameer with a mischievous glint in his eyes.

"You didn't finish your story... who caught you? What happened after that?" asks Preeti.

"One of my classmates, an irritating girl called Lavleen... she used to hate me. She found out about it and snitched to the class teacher. The teacher then searched my bag and boom!" says Sameer, throwing his hands up in the air.

"Then?"

"Nothing much actually. My class teacher, Miss Navneet, loved me. I was always among the top five in class and her pet. She just yelled at me in front of the class, then later pulled me aside. She was like, 'I won't inform the principal or your parents, don't worry. You give me these magazines. But this is our secret, okay? You should not tell anyone about this, A-N-Y-O-N-E, understood? No one should come to know that I kept your magazines, okay?' Then she rolled the magazines and put them in her purse. She must have had a good, good na-aa-aight," says Sameer in a sing-song tone and laughs aloud.

Preeti lets out an incredulous gasp. "What? Your female teacher kept your stash of dirty mags?"

"Yeah, and she was hot too," says Sameer dreamily.

"That is wrong on so many levels!"

"Whatever!"

"Did you even understand what was going on at that point?"

"Nah! But I did a few years later. Anyway, enough about me. I have been meaning to ask you something for a few days now."

"Go on," says Preeti.

"Don't feel bad, okay?"

"You are getting too dramatic now," says Preeti.

"Can I look at your paintings?" he asks.

"Of course!" says Preeti without a moment's consideration or thought.

She walks into her bedroom with Sameer right behind her, their plates still in hand.

"This is insane!" exclaims Sameer as he steps into the room.He looks around, overwhelmed by the sheer number of paintings lining the floor. He sits down in front of one of the paintings and puts his plate on the floor right next to him. "This is extraordinary work!" he says earnestly, looking up just in time to meet Preeti's eyes. She has a big smile on her face.

"Thanks a lot, Sameer!"

He pauses in frontof a canvas and looks up at Preeti, "Is it fine if I take a closer look?"

"Of course, it's okay!"

He holds up the painting at arm's length and after several minutes, finally speaks, "You know what? You should have an exhibition of your works."

"Stop joking again. I'm not that good," says Preeti.

"That's what you think."

"I know you are trying to be supportive and I appreciate that, but really, come on," says Preeti.

Sameer lets out a sigh of exasperation.

"Sorry, mama! I have been really busy. This new project is so fuc...frustrating," says Preeti, responding to her mother's complaint that she hasn't heard from her daughter in a while.

Preeti has been cut off from everyone. She hasn't even met Sameer or any of her other friends since the start of her new project at work. She leaves for office early in the morning and reaches home by eleven at night. She last met Sameer when he came over to her apartment for dinner the previous week and looked at her paintings. WhatsApp messages have been their only mode of communication.

"Yes mama, I have been eating properly," lies Preeti and continues to placate her mother's worries.

"Bye mama, good night," says Preeti and closes the door of the lift. She drags her tired feet to her apartment, looking forward to the weekend so she can catch up on some sleep. Preeti is about to take her keys out when she notices that her apartment door is slightly open and the living room lights are switched on. Preeti freezes on the spot for a moment, her mind running blank, unsure what to do next. She is about to push the door open, but retracts her hand. Getting a grip on her nerves, she tiptoes to Sameer's apartment and rings his doorbell, her eyes on her apartment all the while.

"Hey!" says Sameer cheerfully as he opens the door.

"Shh..." says Preeti, pressing her fingers to her lips and pointing at her apartment with her other hand.

Sameer gestures as if to ask, "What?"

Preeti steps inside and whispers in his ears, "I think someone has broken into my apartment. The door was open when I arrived."

Sameer whispers, "Oh, finally a real thief, eh? Let me handle this," before walking into his bedroom and coming out with a cricket bat.

"What are you doing?" whispers Preeti.

"If the thieves are still there," he pauses to raise his bat in the air and says, "they will get some of this."

"Are you bloody insane? God knows who these people are, they might have knives or something worse..." says Preeti, struggling to keep her voice down.

"I will be fine," says Sameer.

"Don't act stupid. Let me call the security guard..." she says and starts dialling the number.

"By the time the guard comes here, the thieves would have already left with your stuff. Let me handle this. You stay here. If something happens, I will raise my voice, you can call security then. Got it?"

"This is not a good idea..."

"Trust me."

"Fine," says Preeti hesitantly.

Sameer takes off his shoes and silently walks into Preeti's apartment. She stands behind the door of his house, alert and nervous. After two minutes, when she doesn't hear anything, she starts to get anxious and steps outside. She pushes open the door of her apartment with cautious steps.

"Bahhhhh..." Sameer jumps at her from behind the door.

"Mamaaaaa! No!" Preeti screams, throwing her purse on the ground and hiding her face behind her hands.

"Hahahaha!" Sameer guffaws.

"It's not funny, Sameer," Preeti grumbles.

"I'm sorry, really... I couldn't stop myself from scaring you. I checked everything, no one is here. Looks like you forgot to lock the door and switch off the lights before you stepped out," Sameer says still grinning.

"Not possible. I never do that!" Preeti argues.

"You want to check your stuff?" Sameer asks, deciding to indulge her.

"I think...wait a minute. Why is that door open? I always lock the gallery," Preeti says and rushes forward.

"Oh my god! Oh no... what the hell!" Preeti shouts, throwing open the door to the gallery.

"Hey, what happened?" Sameer asks, following her into the room.

"They took my paintings!" Preeti says, sounding despondent.

"Oh, I'm sorry. I didn't look in this room. I just checked the hall..."

"Why would someone take my paintings?"

"Umm... some fan of yours?"

"Oh, come on... what do I do? This is so wrong... God!"

"Let's check if they took something else."

"Oh yes... shit!" Preeti exclaims and runs towards the bedroom.

"All good there?" Sameer asks.

"Thankfully they didn't touch the almirah. It's still locked... but Sameer, my paintings!"

"Hmm..."

"But why?"

"Maybe some painter heard about you, felt challenged and decided to cut you off before your paintings could wipe out his name," Sameer reasoned.

"Don't be ridiculous, Sameer!" Preeti says, holding her head in her hands.

"I just... I don't believe this!" she says standing up and still looking around the room in surprise. "They took my paintings! What are they going to do with my paintings? Sell them? This does not make any sense!" she says walking over to her cupboards.

"I guess they didn't find anything of value so they took whatever they thought would get them some money," says Sameer.

"I don't know, Sameer... there is something very fishy about this. How did they carry all the paintings? How did no one see them? And the lock isn't broken... how did they get in? You didn't lose the spare key to my apartment, did you?"

"No, I have it with me."

"I can't make head or tail of this. Why did they target my apartment? I feel really scared right now... I'm going to call the police."

"Hey! Calm down, relax. Take a deep breath," says Sameer putting his arm around her shoulder protectively.

"I just can't..." she starts.

"Let's deal with this tomorrow morning, okay?"

"I want to file a police report..."

"What? Right now? It's almost midnight," says Sameer looking at his wristwatch. "Go to sleep right now. You're tired and I know this is a lot to handle, but you need to rest. We will deal with this first thing tomorrow morning. I will come with you."

"But..."

"Preeti, this is a case of theft. The police will easily take a few hours to register an FIR. Let's take care of this in the morning."

"Okay."

"Listen, why don't you come over to my apartment? You can sleep there for the night..."

"No, no, I am fine," she lies. She does not want to admit that she is scared to sleep alone in the same apartment where a thief had broken in only a few hours back.

"Preeti, come over. There's no need to feel awkward."

"I know that, but I'm honestly not scared..."

"Yes, you are. You just said it yourself," says Sameer and drags her out of the door, holding her hand firmly.

◆

"Even now, while bathing, I kept checking behind the shower curtain. I was sure that someone was lurking there in the corner of my house," says Preeti as Sameer drives them to the police station.

"It's only natural for you to feel that way, but at the same time, it is important that you get over it, you know," says Sameer.

"Yeah... hey! You missed the turn. The police station is that way," says Preeti.

"No, we can't take a U-turn here. We will have to take a turn at the next signal," he says.

"What? No! Of course you can take a U-turn."

"I'm telling you, you can't," insists Sameer.

"Fine, whatever," says Preeti.

"Oh great!" says Sameer looking at the traffic congesting the road before the next signal. "There is no way we are going to cross this signal in one go."

"It's okay. It's not like we have an appointment with the police."

"Hmm..."

"Oh, finally!" says Preeti as the traffic starts moving swiftly after the signal goes green the second time.

"What? What are you doing? We were supposed to take a U-turn here now, Sameer!" Preeti shouts.

"Oh! I forgot!"

"What the hell! How can you forget? You just told me a few minutes back. You know what? Let me drive," she says angrily.

"I said I am sorry," he says and steals a glance at his wristwatch.

"Why do you keep looking at your watch?" asks Preeti.

"I just remembered, I have some work at Khar..."

"Do you need to take care of it right now?" asks Preeti.

"Yeah, it's kind of urgent."

"All right. Do me a favour, stop the car. I will get down here and get a cab. I will file the report at the police station and then go home," she says, gritting her teeth.

"I'm so sorry, Preeti. I completely forgot about my other commitment. It's only going to take half an hour, though. Can you accompany me? I will finish my work there, then we'll come back and file the police report."

"What will I do there? No, I'm going to get down here," she says, getting angrier by the minute.

"Come on now, Preeti. You just said it yourself, it's not like we have an appointment with the police. A little delay won't hurt."

"That's not the point, Sameer. It's about you being so damn irresponsible," she says, raising her voice.

"I said I am sorry," he repeats.

Preeti does not answer. After driving for fifteen more minutes, Sameer comes to a halt in front of a modern looking building with white walls.

"Preeti, I have some work here," says Sameer pointing at the board that reads Pradarshak Art Gallery.

"At an art gallery? Have you come here to buy artwork for your home? This is the important work that couldn't wait? This is why we didn't go to the police station first? What the fuck is wrong with you?" says Preeti in a fit of rage.

"No, I'm not here to buy paintings. Preeti, please come with me," he pleads.

Preeti gets out of the car without uttering a word.

They walk in silence. Sameer keeps checking his watch and speaking on his phone.

"Yeah, I am here..." Preeti catches a snippet of his conversation, but is too angry to pay attention.

The minute Preeti steps inside the gallery, she is shocked to see Akshay, Gurav, Tara and Nivi admiring one of the paintings on display.

"This can't be a coincidence," she says looking at Sameer and then walks over to them. "What're you guys doing here?" she asks, patting Nivi and Akshay on their backs.

They turn around.

"Isn't it breathtaking?" asks Tara, gesturing at the painting.

Preeti looks at the painting hung under the soft, yellow light. She has seen it before. It's a silhouette: a haunting landscape of a forest with a spectral figure right at the centre, its back facing the viewer as it observes its surreal surroundings. The circle of infinity stares at her. Preeti gulps, overwhelmed by the sudden realization that Sameer has planned the whole thing. She turns around and looks at him standing quietly, his arms folded, a smile playing on his face.

"This one is my favourite..."says Nivi, standing in front of another painting, a few feet away from the rest of the group. "Come, take a look, Preeti," she adds.

Preeti goes towards Nivi in a daze. She looks at the painting, another of her works. Preeti looks at Sameer and turns her gaze around the gallery adorned with her paintings. She is stunned into silence. The happenings of the previous night come back to her and she realizes what has happened. Sameer's strange behaviour suddenly makes sense.

She walks towards him and says, "I am so… I am so so so sorry, I just… am so sorry… but how? I just can't, I can't believe…" She looks around the gallery at all the unknown faces who seem to be admiring her work in silence. Preeti is overcome by a sense of pride and happiness.

"Never in my wildest dreams did I imagine this, Sameer… how do I thank you? How do I thank all of you?" she says, taking a step forward and hugging Sameer.

"For now, you should be thinking about other things…" says Gurav.

"Like an interview with the *Metro Times*," says Sameer, winking mysteriously.

"Huh? What interview?"

"The one that you are going to give right now," says Akshay.

"What? What are you talking…" Before Preeti can gather her thoughts, a lady in her mid-twenties approaches her. She is accompanied by a young man carrying a camera.

"Hello Miss Preeti Thaker! I am Meghna Sabharwal from *Metro Times* and this is my photographer, Vimal Garg," says the lady, sounding exuberant.

"Hi!" says Preeti, forcing a smile and stealing a look at her friends.

"Congratulations! Your paintings are so deep and marvellously artistic," says Meghna.

"Thanks," says Preeti.

"Before we continue with the interview, let's take a photograph… why don't you stand over there, right next to that painting, yeah, over there..."instructs Meghna. "*Chalega*, right?" she asks turning towards Vimal. He nods.

Preeti takes an uncertain step towards the painting, nervously running her hands through her hair, tucking stray strands behind her ear.

"Ready?" asks the photographer.

Preeti nods and smiles nervously, momentarily looking at Sameer and her friends, and then back at the camera lens.

◆

"You should have seen the look on Preeti's face... she was like, 'I think someone has broken into my apartment'. Her voice was barely above a whisper," says Sameer as he fishes out a *Kingfisher* bottle from the ice bucket.

"How on earth did you manage to keep a straight face?" asks Nivi, momentarily taking her eyes off the handsome guy sitting a few tables away from them.

"*Darshan* ho gaye? Satisfied?" asks Akshay catching her line of sight.

"Not yet!" she says and winks at him.

"Arrey but seriously, his act was so convincing. I thought it was very strange... I mean, why would someone steal my paintings? But I couldn't imagine Sameer having a hand in this," says Preeti.

"Not just his hand, all our hands," says Nivi. "He has been planning this for quite some time..."

"Yeah, we thought it was an outrageous idea," says Gurav.

"We were sure that no art gallery owner would host an exhibition of an unknown artist. Having one or two odd paintings is one thing, but an exhibition. Sameer was determined that he would have it no other way," says Tara and picks up another bottle, her third.

"*Upar* se he also managed to get the exhibition covered by *Metro Times, The Cauldron* and *Mumbai Darshan,*" says Nivi.

"We don't have the slightest clue how. It's all a big mystery, even to us. We did quite a bit of manual labour, though..." Akshay pitches in.

"The minute you left for office that day, we jumped into action. Oh, and by the way, we stayed at Sameer's apartment the night before the 'theft' took place," says Gurav. "We didn't have much time... we needed to remove all the paintings from the house, get them framed, and then take them to the art gallery. Again, we don't have any idea how Sameer managed to convince the art gallery owner..."

"Not to forget that Sameer had been breaking into your house occasionally and sneaking out your paintings one at a time," Tara chips in.

"What?" says Preeti in astonishment, looking at the empty chair where Sameer had been sitting just moments ago.

"I don't believe this!" she says. The minute Sameer walks in, Preeti gets up abruptly, walks over to Sameer and hugs him.

"Thank you so much, Sameer!"

"Err... umm, okay... what is happeni..."

Preeti pulls back and continues as if she didn't hear him at all, "I don't know what to say... no one has ever done anything like this for me before." Her eyes well up and despite the tears that roll down her face, a smile plays on her lips.

"Wah! Wah! We toh don't get any credit only," says Tara.

"Tara!" exclaims Preeti as she squeezes herself into a spot on the couch between Nivi and Tara and hugs them both.

"I have been dreaming about this for a while now," says Gurav.

Everyone bursts out laughing.

Soon their party moves from the pub to Sameer's apartment.

"What do you guys want to do?" asks Sameer.

"Pata nahi," says Preeti munching on wafers.

"Let's play a drinking game... TV chalu kar, Sameer," says Gurav.

"TV dekhega?" Sameer sounds sceptical.

"Do it, yaar!"

Gurav grabs the remote control and surfs a couple of channels before settling on a daily Hindi soap.

"Ae yaar! Are you for real?" asks Tara.

"Seriously!" says Preeti.

"You said that we were going to play a drinking game..." says Akshay.

"Pchch! Will you people listen to me? So, every time one of those actresses start crying, we empty our glasses," says Gurav.

Everyone laughs aloud, especially Tara. "That is bloody genius!" she says.

"I think by the time this show is over, we will all have had enough," says Preeti.

And so the table clutters up with empty beer bottles as they continue to play their game for a few hours, watching one show after the other.

After an hour-and-a-half, Preeti has had enough. "Ga... guys. Ab aur nahi," she stutters.

"Same... ere" says Tara, yawning noisily.

"I toh am sleeping," says Akshay, pushing Gurav and Sameer off the couch with a cushion. He lies down on the couch and covers his face with the cushion.

"*Kya tum log!* I am not... not feeling sleepy," says Gurav and stifles a yawn. "Let's watch something. You have any movie on your laptop kya?" he asks.

"Plenty!" says Sameer and winks mischievously. He gets up and leaves the room to bring his laptop.

"I'm going to fall asleep any moment now," says Tara crouching in a foetal position on the floor, a cushion propped under her head.

Preeti excuses herself and heads to the kitchen to get a glass of water. By the time she comes back, everyone has fallen asleep. Sameer is sitting at the dining table, his laptop in front of him, checking some folders. "Come," he whispers getting up.

Preeti gestures as if to ask, "Where?"

"Can't watch anything here... waise I don't think any of these guys will wake up before ten in the morning," he says softly and gestures towards his bedroom.

Preeti follows him.

As Preeti steps into Sameer's bedroom, she can't help but notice the stark difference between the living and bed room. While the living room is vibrant, this room is sombre. A double bed stands in the middle, decked in off-white sheets. A dark mahogany cupboard stands in a corner next to a study table and a chair. Sameer places the laptop on the bed and sits on the floor. Preeti sits beside him. They browse through his movies folder for several minutes and end up starting a couple of romantic movies, one action movie and a horror movie before deciding that they really don't want to watch anything.

"Sameer, this is for you..." Preeti says, placing a small gift-wrapped parcel on his lap. She had kept it hidden in her handbag and had been waiting for the right opportunity to present itself.

"Hey, what's this?" Sameer asks.

"Just a small thank you for everything you've done for me," Preeti says with a smile.

"I'm going to open it right now," Sameer announces and carefully unwraps the pink wrapping paper to unveil a white polo T-shirt with six different coloured handprints on it.

"Like it?" Preeti asks.

"Man, this has to be framed. All the guys put their hands on this tee?" Sameer asks, holding the T-shirt up to the light.

Preeti nods.

"Your idea?"

Preeti nods again.

"Oh my, thank you, Preeti .. means a lot..." Sameer puts an arm around her waist.

Preeti feels a strange warmth course through her body. She smiles awkwardly.

"So you're a bigshot artist now, huh?" says Sameer as he grabs a pillow and hands another one to Preeti. While she fluffs the pillow on her lap, Sameer lies down beside her on the floor in the space between the bed and the wall.

"Can't wait..." Sameer yawns and says, "for tomorrow."

"Why?"

"Geth chu lead ywar intavoo ennn da newspaper..."

"Ah, the interview... yes! This has been a great day... thank you for believing in me, Sameer. I am, I'm truly blessed to have you in my life. Thank you for letting me be something I wouldn't have dared to be on my own."

"It's me who's blessed... it is my... my honour to have you in my life," he says and turns on his stomach. Propping himself up on his elbows, he looks at Preeti with bloodshot eyes. "I'm very proud of you, Preeti, very proud. Everyone struggles in life, some more than others, but only few turn the tides in their favour. You let your problems make a better person of you, you let it reveal a part of you that is infinite, beautiful. I have not done anything, trust me. It's all you. It has been you all along. I only held up a mirror for you to see what was there. Your challenges have been your opportunities. You are a very special woman, Preeti Thaker, a very, very special woman. Don"t let anyone or anything convince you otherwise," he says and turns on his back again, missing the tears in Preeti's eyes; tears of affection, gratitude and warmth, everything that her frigid fate has long tried to make her forget.

"Sameer, I don't think you could have said anything more beautiful…" Preeti says, moving closer so she can hug him.

"Preeti," Sameer whispers, hugging her back.

"Yes?" Preeti asks, feeling safe in his masculine arms.

"I just did!"

As she realizes what Sameer's words mean, a flush creeps up her cheeks. She pulls away from the embrace, hoping he didn't she her blushing.

After a moment's silence, he says, "You know something, Preeti?"

"Tell me…"

"I love you."

Preeti freezes. The three words register not in her brain, but directly in her heart.

"What?" she asks in disbelief, certain that she has misheard. Her brain shuts down as the words echo within her. Her skin breaks into goosebumps even though she feels like her body is on fire. Her heart screams at her to say it back, but the words don't come out. Did he really hear what she thought she heard? She wonders if it's the liquor that made him say what he did. Or maybe he said something else and she heard it all wrong.

"I love you…"he says, "you are a helluva amazin' person. I love you… my besstttt friend!" and falls asleep.

Preeti feels her racing heart slow down. The word 'friend' booms in her ears. She quietly gets up and leaves the room, and then the apartment.

She is sure of two things by now:
- She is in love with Sameer Arora.
- He is not in love with her.

And she has no clue how to come to terms with both.

◆

5/3/2014

I am in love!

I am in love with Sameer! It's such a strange feeling. Until tonight, I didn't even realize it... I guess the seed was planted a long time back and I didn't notice that the sapling was growing, the leaves sprouting, the roots pushing deeper and stronger, the branches becoming sturdier, and now it has a life of its own. My love has a life of its own. Sameer does not love me the way I love him. Where does that leave me? Should I leave the tree under the sun and wait for the leaves to wilt? How can I do that? How can I let something die? How can I let my love for him die?

That evening, when we were watching that idiotic B-grade movie, Sameer had held my hand while laughing at Akshay's impersonation of the actress. I so wished he wouldn't let go and it was almost as if he had heard me, he had held on to it till the lights came on. Was it then that I became hopeful? No, I think it was even before that. He is unlike any other guy. Should I tell him how I feel? No... no, I can't. Even if I gathered all the guts of my past, present and future selves, I doubt whether I would be able to even utter the first letter of those three words as nonchalantly as he had done. The shadow of my past will always dissect my future. And considering for a moment I get hit by some insane un-Preeti like bolt of 'I'll axe my own heart' kind of courage and I tell him how I feel...then what? I am sure it will spoil everything between us. I will even lose his friendship. I am sure he pitied me after seeing my state and did everything he could to lift me up. I wouldn't want to lose his friendship. He's the closest I've ever been with anyone.

Why can't I just continue to love him regardless of what or how he feels? Why can't I submit myself to selfless love? Will I ever be able to? I don't know. All I know is that it hurts really bad. Such a cruel twist of fate... to heal me and then break me apart all over again.

I want to run to him, right into his arms, but instead, I have to run away, run as fast as I can, as far as I can get away from him. How will I get through this? God, I'm so confused. Please help me. I wish Sameer would realize what he means to me without me ever saying that to him. Can that ever happen, god? Can you make it happen? I wish you knew, Sameer...only if you knew!

"Preeti Thaker wears multiple hats. She is an IT manager who works at Obsoft by day and a gifted wizard with the brush by night..."

Nivi and Akshay read the newspaper article out loud while Sameer, Gurav and Tara sat around the bench, listening in rapt attention. They are at their favourite hangout, having bun maska and tea on a lazy Sunday morning. Preeti is lost in thought. Her eyes are puffy and red. She is unusually quiet and nods every time her friends look at her.

"We are so proud of you!" beams Sameer.

"Absolutely!" says Akshay.

"You bet!" Nivi and Gurav say in unison.

"Hmm, thanks," says Preeti.

"Oh come on, man! You got to give us more than 'hmm'. All your paintings were sold, every single one of them! How many amateur painters can claim to have success like that? Seriously, Preeti, give yourself some credit!"

"Sure," Preeti says quietly.

No one notices her morose demeanour other than Sameer. He does not know what has gotten into Preeti. He does not raise the issue in front of everyone, but makes a mental note to ask her later when no one else is around.

"Now let's discuss the most important thing of all," says Sameer dramatically. "Where is the booty, Preeti? And how do we share it? I am thinking that both of us can keep thirty percent each and these peasants can keep the rest." Sameer knows his comment is bound to crack Preeti up. But her stoic expression does not waver in the slightest.

"Ae hat! Anything! Who are you calling peasants? It's time for a mutiny, my fellow men and women," says Akshay, standing up and dramatically waving his hand.

"Chup re!" says Nivi. "Tell us about your plans, Preeti. Are you going to continue painting? There is a lot of money in it, so you can leave your job too. How exciting is that!"

"No plans as such. I will give away all the money to charity. Those paintings weren't for profit. I made them in my brother's memory. As for quitting my job, I won't. Like I said, painting is not a career option for me."

"You will give it all to a charity? All of it? Whoa!"says Gurav. "I wish I was the managing director of some NGO..."

"That's so noble, Preeti," Sameer cuts in.

"Hmm," says Preeti, getting up abruptly. "I need to go now. I have a lot of laundry to do and some other odd jobs around the house..."

"Arrey! Sit na! What's the hurry?" says Tara.

"No, I have to go," says Preeti.

"We will help you out with your chores, Preeti. We were thinking about going for lunch and then catching a movie," says Nivi.

"See you later, guys, I need to go," says Preeti with an air of finality.

"Okay fine." Sameer gets up. "Let me drop you."

"That won't be necessary. It's just a ten-minute walk," she says politely.

"I have left my credit card and I'm not carrying much cash either. I need to pick it up from my room," Sameer lies. He needs to speak to Preeti. He is disturbed by her unusual behaviour.

"Okay, bye guys!" says Preeti.

"Is everything fine?" asks Sameer the minute they are inside the car.

"I am absolutely fine."

"I couldn't help but notice that you seemed completely off today. I have never seen you like this before. And your eyes are puffy too. I can tell you have been crying."

"Nothing really. I was thinking about my brother," says Preeti looking straight ahead. A part of her wants to tell Sameer how she feels, but she holds back, convinced that nothing good will come out of it.

"You are lying," says Sameer flatly.

"No."

"Preeti..."

"Sameer, I'm not a happy-go-lucky person like you. I don't wake up everyday feeling cheerful and bubbly, wanting to hang out with friends. Just let me be," she snaps at him.

"I am sorry," says Sameer.

They drive in silence till they reach their apartment. Preeti feels terrible for reacting the way she did, but she does not apologize.

◆

In the weeks that follow, Preeti often spends her nights playing out scenarios in her head, imagining how things would turn out if she took either of the options –to pursue Sameer or to leave him. As these emotions churn inside the cauldron of her restless mind, it becomes increasingly difficult for her to be around Sameer. Several times she's decided to tell him how she feels, but when she comes face to face with him, she reconsiders her decision and weighs down what appeared to be a perfectly legitimate reason until a moment ago.

In a desperate bid to put an end to her misery, she tries to back her feelings, attempting to bury them in the folds of her mind, drown them in the murky waters of all the things she has left behind, convince herself that her feelings for him will never be reciprocated. But every attempt feels like running straight into a concrete wall. On the surface, nothing has changed. Sameer is his usual supportive, funny self, unaware that his best friend is in love with him. As hard as it is, Preeti tries to be her usual self too, but she is becoming increasingly aware that she wants a lot more.

It's a Friday night. Preeti is in her apartment browsing Sameer's Facebook profile on her laptop – looking at his photos, occasionally snooping on random women she finds in them. It's one of those days when Preeti is convinced that she and Sameer have a chance, that he too will fall in love with her some day. She wants to make sure there isn't another woman in his life. Preeti knows for a fact that Sameer isn't dating anyone and neither has he had a girlfriend in a long time. But her insecurity is too strong. No matter how old or young, when love happens, it hits you with a shot of childish exuberance. And after all, this is Preeti's first time in love.

Preeti is checking the profile of a certain Aditi Gaekwad who is in Sameer's Facebook friend list and has tagged him in an old photograph in which she is seen clicking a selfie with Sameer and a few others she doesn't recognise. Just then, her phone buzzes. It's Sameer.

Hey Preeti! Ssup?

Preeti's heartbeats climb faster than the elevator at the Burj Khalifa. She reads the ping several times over and imagines hearing Sameer say the words aloud in his smooth voice. After considering carefully what to reply, she types:

Busy. Got a client call in 10 min.

After the first wave of excitement has washed over her and the euphoria dies down, the reality of the situation soaks in. She can't evade it. She needs to avoid Sameer as much as she can. It is the only thing she can do to stay sane.

Ok. Listen, v r planning karaoke nyt 2moro…

Srry, cant mk it. Proj work.Vl be going to ofc…will be thr till midnight

Oh come on! It wont be the same without u.

I really cant Sameer. I am srry.

Ok. Some other time…tc.

◆

"Man, that chick over there is so hot…" says Akshay looking at a woman in a black dress by the bar.

"She is highwaaaaaays out of your league, dude," says Gurav.

Tara guffaws. "Let the man dream… dreams are tax-free," she says.

"What's up with you, Sameer? You've been really quiet," says Nivi.

"Tu bhi! First Preeti, now you, it seems the like disease is contagious," says Akshay, dramatically stroking his chin. Everyone has noticed the change in Preeti's behaviour.

"I can feel a migraine building up. I think I will leave," says Sameer.

"Arrey! You should have told us before…" says Tara.

"No, I didn't want to ruin our plans for the evening…" says Sameer.

"Bakwaas!" says Gurav.

"Chalo then, I will make a move," says Sameer, getting up.

"Chala jayega?" asks Akshay.

"Yeah," says Sameer and walks out.

When Sameer steps out of the elevator, he is surprised to see Preeti's door unlocked. It's only nine in the evening. He remembers Preeti telling him that she would not reach home before midnight. Sameer considers going over to her apartment and checking on her, but changes his mind thinking that she might be working.

◆

It's ten in the morning next day and Preeti has just returned after shopping for groceries from the nearby store. She is about to open the door to her flat when Sameer comes out of his apartment. He has just woken up and has come out to collect the newspaper.

"Hi!" says Sameer, picking up the newspaper and walking towards Preeti.

"Hey!" says Preeti.

"What's up? How's work?" asks Sameer.

"Don't ask! I came home at one last night. My boss is a monster…"

It isn't the lie itself that surprises Sameer as much as the fact that she does not consider him close enough to take into confidence, even about a trivial matter. However, Sameer does not confront her and gives her the benefit of doubt, convincing himself that she must have a very good reason for not telling him the truth.

◆

7/3/2014

This is harder than I thought it would be. They say you should marry the person you are the closest to – the guy with whom you can share your 3 a.m. thoughts. The guy who knows what you want before you open your mouth. The angel who reads your mind before you can articulate your thoughts. The friend you can laugh and cry with. The person who tells you he loves you every night and spends the day proving it through little gestures that speak much louder than any words of love. The person with whom you can hold hands when you turn eighty and announce to the world – "We made it!"

For me that person is Sameer, of this I'm sure. But I'm also sure that I am not the one for Sameer. I'm the meek and unglamorous 'best friend' who has a boring corporate life. He needs a rational and confident woman who speaks her mind and knows what's it like to be romantic as his life partner. That's his type, I can tell. I can never be that. It tears me apart to be in his presence and not be able to tell him how my heart bleeds for him. I'm afraid of meeting his eye, lest he see what lies behind the veil of my pretence. And yet I can't stand being away from him. Sometimes I feel so foolish, so immature. I find myself acting like a teenager. It's such a surge of emotions…

Sometimes I wonder, how will he react if he knows I love him? Would he see me in a different light? Would he want to give his heart to me? I want him to acknowledge my pain, I want him to embrace my madness, I want him to know that I love him, that every part of me is so drenched in this emotion that I am sore, and only his embrace can set me free of this agony…

God! Only if he knew…

◆

Preeti is in a quaint little coffee house, sipping on a cup of mocha and writing in her journal. It's Saturday morning. Sameer and their common friends are out for lunch. Preeti has excused herself, telling them that she is heading to office for urgent work.

9/3/2014

I love this place. I love the smell of coffee that lingers in the air. I love how the charm above the door rings every time someone steps inside. I can sit here all day long and just watch random people on the street, better than being home anyway.

◆

It's four in the afternoon. Preeti is still in the coffee house, reading a book she picked up from the shelf adjoining the wall decked in graffiti. She has had three cups of coffee and umpteen slices of garlic bread.

"...Oh god! My stomach still hurts... the way you tripped in the bowling alley..."

A voice accompanies the *ting-ting* of the bell above the door as a customer steps inside the coffee house.

Engrossed in her book, Preeti is oblivious to the buzz around her. With her back to the door and tucked away in a far corner of the room, she does not realize that the voice belongs to Nivi, who is accompanied by their common friends.

"I don't know what happened... one minute I'm trying to act cool, my focus on the bowling pins, the next minute I'm on the floor, looking at the roof above, the ball still in my hand," says Gurav as he pulls up a chair.

They are all engrossed in the conversation. In the crowded coffee house, they fail to notice Preeti.

"It would have been awesome if Preeti was there too, she would have lost her shit," says Akshay.

"Yeah..." says Sameer and pings Preeti.

Hey! V r all missing u!

Hey!

Where r u?

Sitting in ofc

As Preeti gets up to pick yet another book, Sameer spots her. He loses his cool and slams his hand on the table. He walks over to her in a fit of rage.

"Hello," says Sameer with a grim expression.

Preeti puts her novel down and looks up at him in surprise. "Hi Sameer," she says in a nervous tone. Their friends have noticed them and they walk over to Preeti's table.

"Hi Preeti! What are you doing here? Sameer told us you couldn't join us because you were working," says Tara moving in her direction and giving her a hug.

"Yeah, finished my work earlier than expected, so I came here to kill time..." says Preeti.

"Arrey! You should have called us na!" says Nivi.

"Where is your laptop, Preeti?" asks Sameer in a cold voice.

"Oh! It... is in my car," says Preeti. "Let's just pull a few chairs here..." she says, looking around.

"Yeah... there is one here," says Akshay.

"I'm pretty sure it isn't," says Sameer, looking right at Preeti.

"What?" Preeti pauses in the middle of pulling a chair from the adjoining table.

"I'm pretty sure your laptop is not in your car," says Sameer.

"What do you mean?" asks Preeti.

"I mean that your laptop is not in your car because you never went to office," says Sameer.

"What are you saying, Sameer? Why would I lie to you guys? Of course I went to office," she says.

"Since when did you start carrying your journal to the office?" he asks.

"I do, sometimes..."

"Preeti, please stop lying. You are making a fool out of yourself. For god's sake, I just pinged you, and you replied that you were in office..." says Sameer, his voice rising. The couple at the next table shoots them a dirty look.

"Sameer, abhi nahi," says Gurav, trying to calm him down.

"Arrey yaar! I don't know what her problem is...why is she lying to me? If she didn't want to come, she should have said so," Sameer says angrily.

"Chhod na!" says Akshay.

"Nahi yaar! I've been observing her for the last few weeks now and I know that even you guys have... she has been acting weird since the day after the exhibition at the art gallery. She has been lying for petty reasons..."

He turns towards Preeti and says, "The other night when we went to the karaoke place, I came home early and I know you were in your apartment because your door was unlocked. But when we saw each other the next morning, you lied that you had come home after midnight. Look, if you don't want to spend time with us, fine! It's not as if our world will come crashing down on us if you don't, but quit being immature."

Preeti is quiet. She knows it's all her fault, but she does not know what to say. She has never heard Sameer raise his voice before. She has never seen him angry. She blanks out, unable to gather her thoughts. She doesn't know how to respond to his anger. She quietly picks up her journal and pen, and tucks a five hundred-rupee note under her half-empty cup of mocha.

"Preeti..." says Tara.

"No, let her leave. She needs to take her drama elsewhere," says Sameer.

Preeti leaves the coffee house, a flood of tears straining against her eyelids.

11/3/2014

Did you ever wish that you had a second chance to meet someone again for the first time? I wish I had that chance now. I have destroyed everything. I can't have his love. And now I have ruined our friendship too. I really want to fix this somehow. But how? It is my fault. I wanted more. I became selfish. And now I am left with nothing.

We were in the apartment lift this morning together and he didn't say a word, not a single word. I couldn't stand it. I couldn't stand sharing that space with him as a stranger.

I don't know how long it's going to be this way. I know for certain that there's nothing I can do. What will I tell him? How will I justify all the silly lies? How will he react if I tell him I lied because I was trying to stay away from him in order to suppress my feelings? Won't that change everything? But everything has changed already and it's all my fault.

◆

It's a bright Monday morning. Preeti's society members have gathered in their lawns to play Holi. Preeti is there too. She didn't want to, but ten minutes before the function, kids from the society had barged into her flat, dragging her to the lawns. Dressed in a white salwar kameez and holding a polythene bag full of different colours, she goes around the lawn greeting the other members and applying gulaal to their faces. She even puts some colour on the arrogant watchman, who smiles at her in an awkward manner. Holi is the time to forgive and forget, to forge new bonds and renew old ones. Her own face is barely recognizable, caked as it is under layers of red and yellow colour.

"Happy Holi!" says a familiar voice as a pair of hands reach out to smear blue colour all over her face.

Preeti feels a warm quivering sensation spread through her as she turns around to see Sameer. For a second she freezes and then seeing that smile she knows so well, she feels her insides warm up. The warmth spreads all the way up to her face. "Paint her green now!" Nivi shouts.

Sameer dumps a handful of green colour over her. In response, Preeti smears gulaal all over his face. They hug.

"Are we okay now?" asks Sameer, who has decided he has had enough of his best friend's tantrums.

"Yes, we are," says Preeti breaking into a shy smile. "I am sorry for the way I behaved..."

"Shh, don't apologize, Preeti. Let's pretend that nothing ever happened—"

They don't get an opportunity to finish their conversation as their friends join them.

"Happy Holi, Preeti!" says Gurav, smearing yellow colour all over Preeti's hair.

"No, not the hair... I just shampooed..." Preeti protests but soon Akshay, Nivi and Tara join and colour her hair, making her look like a rainbow-coloured leprechaun.

"Argh!"They yell in unison as Sameer empties a bucket of cold water over their heads.

"War!" yells Gurav as he takes an empty bucket and runs to fill it from a tap near the garden.

Akshay hands out water balloons to Tara, Nivi and Preeti and they chase Sameer around the garden, trying to hit him with the balloons. Preeti manages to pelt him on his behind. Sameer stops and glares at Preeti in a comic manner.

"Oops, I'm sorry..." Preeti mutters and backtracks on seeing Sameer rush towards her.

Gurav returns with a bucket of water and throws it at Sameer, who ducks. Gurav ends up soaking Nivi instead.

"Gurav *ke bachche*!" Nivi yells, and throws a water balloon at him.

Gurav ducks and says, "Arrey, I was trying to throw water at Sameer, not you, yaar!"

"He is lying, Nivi, don't leave him aise hi!" laughs Sameer, catching hold of Preeti and tickling her ribs.

"Stop, stop... time please!" Preeti shouts, her face turning red.

Smack!

Gurav gets hit in the face with a water bailoon.

"Bull's eye!" yells Tara and laughs aloud as Gurav smarts from the hit, rubbing his face with his hands.

"Chalo yaar, I am feeling hungry now," says Akshay looking at the table loaded with delicacies in one corner of the garden.

"By the way, did I tell you that you look beautiful in white? I'm sorry we ruined the dress," says Sameer to Preeti.

She blushes furiously. "Thanks!" she says.

"I missed you," Sameer says abruptly, looking straight into her eyes.

Preeti doesn't reply for a moment, taking in the gravity of his words. "I did too."

"But if I didn't say so, you wouldn't have either, no?"

"I... no, I would... I..."

"It's okay, Preeti, I was just taking your case," he grins.

"Man, these *bhajiyas* are just awesome!" says Akshay, stuffing his mouth.

"I know, right?" says Tara shoving a few into her mouth.

"Have you guys tried the *thandai* yet?" asks Gurav, taking a sip from a steel glass.

"It has to be *bhaang,* not *thandai,*" says Nivi, looking at the drink suspiciously.

"Yeah sure, like you wouldn't touch that stuff if it was bhaang," says Tara as she pours the drink into a glass and mixes two spoons of the powder-like substance from the bowl next to the jug.

"Arrey, don't you think you added a bit too much of that stuff?" asks Akshay.

"Who says it's for me?" she says and winks at him while she makes another drink. "There you go guys," says Tara, handing over the glasses to Preeti and Sameer as they finally join them.

Balam pichkaari, jo tune mujhe maari...

The DJ belts out a popular track from a Bollywood movie. Akshay and Nivi start dancing. Soon they are joined by other society members. The rest of the group follows. The DJ plays one popular Holi song after another. Everyone keeps refilling their glasses, their steps becoming more and more shaky. Preeti gestures to the rest of the group that she is going to get another refill. She has had two glasses of bhaang till now while the others have had as many, if not less.

Preeti staggers her way towards the table when *Rang barse* starts playing. She feels someone tugging at her dupatta from behind. She turns around to see Sameer holding it in a tight grip. "*Bheege chunar wali*," Sameer mouths the words and starts pulling her dupatta towards him. Preeti blushes furiously.

"Sameer!" she opens her eyes wide and gestures as if to ask "what are you doing?"

"Sameer, let go!" she whispers, trying hard to keep her voice down.

Sameer lets go of her and slumps on the grass.

"*Bheege chunar wali*" he keeps singing over and over, oblivious to everyone watching him.

"*Chad gayi bhaang*!" says Gurav and sticks his hand under Sameer's armpit, trying to pull him up. Akshay supports him from the other side and together they take him up to his apartment. Nivi, Tara and Preeti follow.

"That shit was strong!" says Akshay as they enter Sameer's living room.

"The bloody room is spinning," says Tara holding her head between her hands as she eases herself onto the couch.

"I feel... I don't know... I feel... weird," says Preeti settling on the floor next to Tara and resting her head on her knees.

"You guys want to play something? Truth or dare?" asks Gurav.

"Are you in high school or what? Truth or dare!" Nivi says contemptuously.

"Sounds good to me," says Preeti.

"It's a dumb game," says Nivi flatly.

"Okay, let's take a vote," says Akshay.

After a quick show of hands, it is decided that they will play truth or dare.

"We are ready," says Gurav as he walks out of the kitchen and into the living room with an empty beer bottle in his hand.

"We will start from Akshay and go clockwise," says Gurav handing him the bottle.

"Akshay, start now!" says Nivi.

"Okay, here goes," he says and spins the bottle.

The head of the bottle comes to rest on Nivi.

"Truth!" she says promptly.

"Chicken!" mocks Tara.

"Umm... let's see..."says Akshay. "Any ideas, guys?"

"Ask her something about Deepesh..." Gurav ponders aloud, referring to one of her ex-boyfriends whom they all hated.

Nivi shoots him a dirty look.

"Fine, fine! No questions about anyone's exes, okay?" Gurav declares.

"Kya yaar! Fine... have you ever fancied a woman?" asks Akshay.

After a moment's silence, Nivi replies, "Yes!"

"Whoa!" says Sameer and sits up straight. "The game just got super interesting!"

"Tharki!" says Tara.

"Tell us who? Is it someone we know?" Preeti asks Nivi.

"I am not answering any of those questions. We are only asking yes or no questions," says Nivi.

"Arrey come on yaar! Bata na!" says Sameer.

"I'm not saying anything more," says Nivi.

"Such a spoilsport. Let's move ahead now. Sameer, your turn," says Tara.

Sameer spins the bottle and after a few moments, it comes to rest at Gurav. Sameer flashes a malicious grin and without a moment's thought asks, "When was the last time you got laid?"

"That was fast..." Preeti wonders aloud.

"Sameer's brain works faster than Chacha Chaudhary's in these matters," says Tara.

"What the hell? What happened to only yes or no questions?" says Gurav in Nivi's voice.

"Quit being a five-year-old, yaar... and that applies to everyone," says Tara irritably, looking at Nivi. "If everyone has got an exhaustive list of questions that they don't want to be asked, then we might as well play something else..."

"Don't get hyper," says Gurav cutting her short. "Ten months back," he adds quietly.

Everyone bursts out laughing.

"The pain in his voice... oh man!" exclaims Akshay, wiping his tears.

"But ten months is still commendable..." says Sameer.

"I know, right?" says Nivi. Then she looks at Gurav and continues, "I mean, look at you, you look like a homeless man who illegally sells *ganja* on the streets."

Gurav strokes his thick, bushy beard and flattens the untidy mop of slightly curly hair on his head, feeling conscious. "You know nothing, Nivi. Women love my appearance," he says defiantly.

"Oh! You mean the ones you pay, right?" says Nivi.

"Whoa! Burn!" says Preeti and cracks up.

"That was brutal!" says Akshay and raises his hand to high-five her while Preeti spins the bottle.

"Tara!" Preeti exclaims as the bottle comes to rest pointing at her.

"Oh boy! Tara, Preeti is going to slay you," says Sameer sarcastically.

"Yeah, she will probably ask her whether she loves pav bhaji more or vada pav," says Gurav amid peals of laughter.

"Or even worse, she might ask her what her favourite colour is," says Akshay and guffaws.

Sameer flings a cushion at Akshay. "Lame!"

"Shut up guys, let me think," says Preeti. "Err… I can't think of anything. Ideas?"

"What Preeti!" Nivi remarks.

"Wait, I will tell you…" says Sameer and slides beside Preeti. He slips his arm over her shoulder and pulls her gently towards himself so that his lips are close to her ears and his hand is grazing her collarbone. As he whispers into her ears, his warm breath seeps through her skin and ignites a fire inside her. In that moment, Preeti forgets all about the game and everything fades out of her vision. It seems like it's just the two of them in the room. Her thoughts have barely had a chance to spin a yarn when Sameer moves away, grinning.

"I think Preeti is going to take another year before she thinks of a question," says Tara, breaking Preeti's chain of thought.

"Huh?" says Preeti, snapping out of her reverie. "Oh haan! So, umm, Tara, do you have a thing for Gurav?"

"What?" Tara exclaims and looks at Gurav awkwardly. "Hell no! Are you insane?"

Everyone else sniggers. Everyone except Gurav knows that Tara has always liked him.

"All right. Next," says Akshay quietly.

"What? I said I don't have a thing for Gurav," says Tara loudly.

"We all heard that. It's Sameer's turn now."

"Why were you being sarcastic then?"

"Not at all."

"Guys, I am serious. I only like Gurav as a friend."

"Yeah, we heard you!" Akshay and Nivi say in unison.

"Sameer, you asshole, I'm going to kill you, just wait," Tara hisses at Sameer.

"Guys, let's watch a movie or something. I'm getting bored of this game," says Preeti.

"You are just scared that it will be your turn next and your dark secrets will be revealed to all of us," says Gurav, flashing her a wicked smile.

"Please..." starts Preeti, only to be interrupted by Akshay.

"Seriously, I am feeling dead sleepy."

"I thought I was the only one..." says Nivi.

"Same here. I think it's because of the bhaang or something, I don't know... I can barely keep my eyes open," says Gurav stifling a yawn.

"So... what are we doing then?" asks Sameer.

"I don't know about you guys, but I'm going to sleep," declares Akshay, standing up.

"Where are you going?" asks Gurav.

"To Sameer's room."

"Oye! You aren't going anywhere near my bed like this," says Sameer, pointing at Akshay's dirty clothes.

"Oh man! Fine, whatever! I will sleep here then," says Akshay, grabbing a cushion.

"Me too," says Nivi, lying down on the couch and covering her face with a cushion.

Gurav lies down on the floor beside the couch. Within minutes, the living room echoes with their snores.

"Now what?" whispers Tara.

Preeti merely shrugs her shoulders.

"You have ganja?" Tara asks Sameer casually.

"Yeah."

"What?" Preeti asks in surprise. "Ganja, as in the drug? You do drugs, Sameer?"

Tara and Sameer look at each other and smirk.

"Yeah, sometimes."

"Are you kidding me?" asks Preeti. She is convinced that Sameer is lying.

"No."

"Since when?"

"Since college."

"How come I never knew about this?"

"Never really came up..."

Preeti turns towards Tara and asks, "You knew about this?"

Tara guffaws and nods her head. "You have never tried ganja before, have you?" she asks Preeti.

"No."

"Today you will," says Sameer and leads them towards his room.

"But... is it safe? I mean, I don't know," says Preeti as she follows Sameer, with Tara walking alongside her.

"Leave it to the experts..." says Tara, throwing her arm around Preeti, "...kid."

While Tara and Preeti settle on the floor beside the bed, Sameer takes out a thin paper packet from the closet.

"Well, there's always a first time for everything," he says and winks at Preeti while handing Tara a thin, translucent piece of paper.

"What's that?" asks Preeti.

"We are going to use this to make a joint, roll it with that stuff inside," says Tara, pointing at the brown powder-like substance in the paper packet that Sameer has opened and laid on the floor.

"Sort of like a cigarette," says Sameer as he starts rolling a joint himself.

Preeti watches them both keenly.

"Can you hand me the matchbox?" Tara asks Preeti.

"Yeah."

Tara lights up the joint and takes a long puff. Exhaling a huge cloud of smoke, she hands the matchbox to Sameer.

"Your turn." She passes the joint to Preeti.

"This is how you do it," says Sameer. "Hold the joint between your teeth, yeah... inhale, and..." He exhales audibly.

Preeti starts coughing violently as she ingests the smoke instead of exhaling. Sameer pats her back and says, "It's okay, it'll take a few attempts before getting it right."

By the time Preeti recovers, Tara has already finished her joint and started rolling another.

"What on earth...?" Preeti says, genuinely surprised.

"Tara is a total gangster," says Sameer and laughs. "One time she smoked seven joints all by herself, and it was some of the strongest shit I have ever smoked.She got the stuff from Hampi. Akshay and Gurav couldn't go past their third."

Preeti takes a drag and gets it right this time.

"You are a fast learner!" exclaims Sameer.

"Feel anything yet?" asks Tara.

"No, I can taste this weird burnt, bitter flavour on my tongue. I don't see the point of this..."

"It will take a few more puffs before you can see the point, darling," says Tara and laughs aloud.

She continues to smoke joints in rapid succession while Preeti and Sameer take it slow.

With a hint of conspiracy in her voice, Tara says softly, "You know the question you asked me... about Gurav..."

"Yes," says Preeti.

"I lied," she says and grins. She flops her head backwards on the mattress of the bed behind her and continues to smoke in silence while Sameer and Preeti look at each other and smile.

"I am feeling strange..." says Preeti, breathing out a huge cloud of smoke.

"Describe strange," says Sameer.

"The room is spinning very, very slowly..."

"And it feels like everything else is moving fast..." Tara blows rings of smoke and looks up at the ceiling.

"Yeah... like we are talking too fast..."

"You are high," says Sameer.

"Do you see the point of this now?" asks Tara and laughs.

"I, I just want everything to slow down, to shut down... my life, my thoughts, everything... what's the point of all this rush?" says Preeti dreamily.

"You are definitely high," says Sameer.

"Preeti, tell me something..." says Tara, her eyes still grazing the ceiling.

"Hmm."

"Your turn never came, and I wanted to ask you a question..."

"Go on."

"Do you like someone from our group?"

Preeti laughs awkwardly. "What? No! Of course not!"

"It's okay, you can tell us, we'll probably forget everything by tomorrow morning anyway," she says, her eyes tightly shut.

"There is nothing to tell, Tara."

"So you don't like anyone? Hmm... not even him?"

"Who?"

Preeti's question is met with silence as Tara starts to snore. A part of her is relieved that Tara never answered her question, but another part is horrified that Tara has seen through her charade. Then surely the rest of the group must have noticed it as well. Suddenly, the silence in the room appears to shriek into her ears as she realizes that it is just the two of them. Preeti continues to look at Tara, not knowing what to say or do, afraid that Sameer has the same question on his mind. She does not dare to look at him, scared that he will read her mind.

"Preeti," whispers Sameer.

Her heart thumps so loudly that she fears he'll hear it. "Yes," she says timidly, mustering up the courage to look at him.

"Let's go."

"What? Where?"

"To your place. We will smoke there... let Tara sleep here," he says simply.

Preeti heaves a sigh of relief and nods, "Yeah, okay."

They tiptoe out of his apartment and head straight to Preeti's. They skip her sparsely furnished living room and go to her bedroom instead. Sameer starts to lay down his stash on the floor.

"Sameer, we can sit on the bed," she says and smirks.

Sameer smiles sheepishly and hops on the bed. He takes a good, long look around the room. He still remembers all the paintings that once lay stacked on the floor.

"I miss... I miss the paintings, they added so much colour to the room," he says.

"You and I are adding enough colour to it," says Preeti, adjusting her dupatta,which is still damp.

Sameer laughs aloud and starts to roll a joint.

"Let me try one," says Preeti, taking the cigarette paper from his hands.

"Don't take Tara's words seriously, she was high," he says abruptly.

"I know." Preeti is trying to sound as calm as she possibly can.

"Hmm... yeah, that's right," says Sameer as Preeti finishes rolling the joint. "There you go," he says, lighting up.

As Preeti hands over the joint to Sameer after taking a drag, he casually lies down on her lap. Preeti almost stops breathing as she feels the back of his head touch her thigh through her damp clothes. She freezes. Every bit of her is thrown into a pleasant frenzy. It is excruciating. It is exhilarating. There is pleasure in the anarchy.

"I seriously missed you," he says, looking up at her.

Preeti smiles awkwardly, too weak for words.

"Anyway, let's continue the game, yeah?" He takes a puff, his voice getting softer and softer, his drooping eyelids dictating their terms to him.

"Hmm."

"Okay then," he says. "Tell me about your first love."

"Never had one," says Preeti, preparing to roll another joint.

"What? What rubbish, Preeti!"

"What? I'm telling you the truth."

"You've been single all your life?"

"Yeah."

"Must have had a crush at least..."

"No," she lies.

"I don't believe you."

Preeti shrugs.

"Have you ever been kissed?"

"It's supposed to be my turn, Sameer."

"Come on! Forget the game... this is turning out to be a great conversation," he says.

"Stop making excuses to evade your turn."

Sameer lets out a sigh. "Fine!" he says.

"Have you ever done anything illegal?" asks Preeti.

"Yeah," he says casually and breathes out a cloud of smoke.

"Tell me..." Preeti says eagerly.

"I once did Cannabis and drank a shitload of alcohol and got caught by the police while driving..."

"Oh my god! Then?"

"Then I had to spend the night at the police station."

"You are kidding me!"

"No."

"You are so full of surprises!" she says, taking another puff.

"All right, now my turn. Truth it is. Have you ever been kissed?"

"Nah."

Sameer looks at her with his jaws wide open. "My god!"

"I'm serious," says Preeti.

"Well..." he starts.

"I know what you are going to say."

"I'm pretty sure you don't," he says, breaking into a sly smile. "I dare you to kiss a guy."

"What?" Preeti laughs.

"Kiss-a-guy."

"What rubbish! Where will I find a guy now? And secondly, it's my turn, not yours."

"Where will you find a guy to kiss...," he says and pulls her close. "You tell me."

Preeti looks down at Sameer. The smile on his face has disappeared. The intensity of his eyes rips through her being and sets free what she has kept caged till now. Surreal as it seems, she continues to look into his eyes, surrendering to the loud silence, free falling, not knowing when or if she will touch the ground at all. Preeti feels her chest heave and her breath turn ragged. She smiles nervously, unsure if Sameer is thinking the same thing as her. Sameer's expression remains unchanged, his look still as intense, his eyes full of want.

Still lying in her lap, he puts his hands on either side of her face and gently pulls her towards himself.

Preeti is water in his hands. She succumbs to his every whim. As she moves closer, her hair covers Sameer's face, like curtains are being drawn around them. Together, they lose themselves in the darkness that surrounds them, a darkness brighter than any light Preeti has known.

Sameer pauses as the tips of their noses meet, letting them both feel the warmth of each other's breath. Preeti puts her trembling hands on his chest and feels his galloping heart. Sameer gently caresses her cheeks, tracing her face with his thumbs, their lips yearning to meet.

"Don't Sameer, please," she begs.

Sameer smiles and pulls her in. As their lips meet and hopelessly try to quench their thirst, Preeti feels her body explode. She tries to keep her eyes open, but is taken prisoner by the maddening euphoria of the moment. As she feels Sameer's lips glide over hers, as his tongue parts her lips and finds its way inside her moth, restlessly exploring every inch of her with a delicious wetness, Preeti falls further into the arms of ecstasy. An unknown, unexplored world greets her as she envisions all the dreams she had imprisoned in the deep recesses of her brain.

Sameer's hands are caught in the tangles of her hair. Stroking her head gently, he continues to pull her towards himself, making sure there are no distances left to cover. Preeti continues to trace Sameer's chest with her hands, careful not to move beyond his waist. Sameer takes his hand off the back of her head and guides her hands to his trackpants. She fumbles uncertainly, feeling shy, but Sameer continues to press her hand down until she moans into his mouth with unbridled pleasure as she feels him rise in her hands. Sameer gets up at this point, his hands never letting go.

"You want to do this?" he asks, looking straight into her eyes.

Preeti nods, her movements guided by the million emotions zipping through her heart.

"There is something I must tell you, Sameer," she says, her eyes brimming full.

"I know you haven't done this before, Preeti," Sameer says, kissing her cheeks.

"Not that... I don't know how to say... I... I... when I was a kid, I was molested by a school teacher... you know..."

"Say no more." Sameer takes her in his arms, soothing her with his warmth. Sitting on the bed on his knees, he pulls her gently and kisses her soft lips for a long time. When Preeti leans in further, he takes off her dupatta. Standing upright on their knees, they wrap their arms around each other as tightly as they can and continue to kiss. Sameer slides his hands under her kurta. The moment his hand makes contact with her bare waist, she moans once more, her defences completely shattered.

"Sameer… take me!" she cries.

He takes off her kurta, flings it aside and traces her body with his hands, making careful note of every curve, every mole, every perfection, every flaw. He gently lays her on the bed and glides on top of her, this time tracing her waist and stomach with his lips. Helpless moans and passionate cries echo through the room as Preeti feels Sameer's hot breath on her skin. Beads of sweat run down her chest.

Sameer moves upwards, slowly nibbling her skin. His hands are on the cups of her bra, trying to find a way in. As he moves closer, her breath becomes shorter and faster. Sameer slides his hands under her arched back and unhooks her bra. Preeti shivers as he takes it off and buries his face between her breasts. As he kisses them tenderly, she lets out a sigh of pleasure. "Oh, Sameer!"

He loses himself completely in her skin.

He moves up to kiss her once more, holding her hands tightly over her head. His hands slide down, this time finding their way below her waist. He unties the drawstrings of her salwar and removes it. Preeti draws her legs close, feeling conscious.

"It's okay, Preeti. You know I won't hurt you."

Sameer gently looks up at her with a gaze that soothes her apprehensions. He removes his T-shirt and chucks it on the floor and begins lowering his track pants. Preeti takes in his bare muscular body. He puts his lips over her underwear and kisses her gently before sliding his fingers inside and removing them. Sliding down his underwear in one swift motion, Sameer positions himself over her body and begins to kiss her again.

Preeti grabs on to the edges of the bed as she feels Sameer slowly make his way inside her, watching him with eyes half shut, biting her lips every time pain and pleasure collide at the sweet spot she never knew existed.

Sameer looks at her with a glazed expression, the heady cocktail of drugs and testosterone in his body send him into a tizzy. The bed creaks louder and louder with the gradual crescendo of their colliding bodies, their sweaty skin slipping over each other, erasing any friction that had ever existed between them.

"Ah! Sameer!" Preeti yells helplessly. Overwhelmed by the strange, warm, electric sensation that is beginning to spread through her body, she is certain that she is about to scatter into a million pieces. She feels a storm building up inside her abdomen, waiting to be released as she watches Sameer's torso rise and fall above her.

"Sameer, yes! Oh my god… yes… god…" she almost screams and her eyes shut involuntarily. Sameer steals a kiss on her lips and keeps going, rising and dipping into her entire being.

"Look at me!" he says breathlessly.

She opens her eyes just in time to see Sameer's body convulse uncontrollably while she lets go of herself, unable to hold back the flood that is drowning her. A powerful jolt runs through her body as her back arches, pulling all of Sameer inside her. "Oh god!"

"Sameer, I… I… I love you!" The words escape Preeti's lips effortlessly this time.There is no holding back. Not anymore.

"I love you too…"

"Oh Sameer…"

"… Revathy!" he finishes and collapses on top of Preeti.

The euphoria of the moment instantly drains from Preeti's body. For a moment, she does not know how to react. She wonders if she has heard him right.

"What? What did you just say, Sameer?"

"Hmm... Reva," he says.

Preeti's eyes well up with tears. This was supposed to be their moment, just the two of them. This was supposed to be perfect and it had felt that way until a few seconds ago. But now she feels cheated. All her emotions collide against each other.

"Sameer?" she says, her body going cold.

He lies still, not uttering a word.

"Sameer?"

"Hmm." The drowsiness in his voice is evident.

"Sameer, who is Revathy?"

"Hmm, Revathy..."

"Sameer, I want to know who Revathy is," she raises her voice this time, fury bubbling within her.

"Wife..."

"What? Whose wife?"

"My wife."

Preeti pushes Sameer off and gets up. She stands in silence for several minutes, tears fogging her view, her bare body folding unto itself in humiliation.

"Sameer, you are married?" she yells.

Sameer lies still, his chest rising and falling softly.

"Sameer, talk to me! You can't do this to me!" she says and shakes him up.

He does not respond. He is fast asleep.

Her body shivers like a leaf. Preeti picks up her dupatta and wraps herself in it.

She flops down on the floor beside the bed and buries her face in her hands, sobbing. "No one has ever made me feel as low as you have done today, Sameer," she sobs, "and I will never forgive you for that."

Tears stream down her cheeks as she picks up her clothes and heads to the shower.

◆

"Hmm..." Sameer mumbles as he wakes up all of a sudden.

He's still in Preeti's room. It's eight in the evening. A faint glimmer of light tries to penetrate the dark room through the heavy curtains. Sameer has a blinding headache and he barely remembers the events of the afternoon. He looks around in confusion, his eyes trying to adjust in the darkness, the unfamiliar forms of the objects around him adding to the confusion. He tries to get up but falls back on the bed, exhausted and dizzy.

He remains still for several minutes, trying hard to retrace the events before he ended up in this unfamiliar place. He vaguely remembers smoking a joint with Preeti and Tara in his house and then his mental faculties shutting down. He finally manages to get up and fumbles in the dark to find a switch. He turns on the light and realizes that he is in fact in Preeti's room. It confuses him even further: why is he sleeping half-naked in Preeti's room?

He finds his t-shirt neatly folded in a corner of the bed. On top of it is a handwritten note next to a bunch of keys. *Please lock the main door on your way out.*

Shit! She saw me like this...

Sameer puts on the t-shirt, his mind working furiously, trying to remember what happened. He wrings his memory, trying to eke out the events of the afternoon. As he totters back to his apartment, he makes up his mind to speak to Preeti about it.

When Sameer enters his apartment, he finds his friends still asleep. Only Tara is up. She is wide awake and sitting cross-legged on the dining chair, fidgeting with her phone while eating a biscuit.

"Hey!" she whispers.

Sameer joins her, his head still hurting.

"Where were you? Where is Preeti?" she asks.

"What was the last thing we did?" he asks ignoring her questions.

"How would I know?" she says with an amused expression on her face.

"I mean... we were here, the three of us..." he says uncertainly.

"You, me and Preeti smoked a few joints here, and then I fell asleep after some time. When I woke up, you guys weren't here."

"Hmm..."

"What's wrong?"

"Nothing."

"Where is she?"

"I don't know... I fell asleep at her place. When I woke up, she was not there. She must have gone out to get something, I don't know."

"Are you sure everything is fine?"

"Yeah... I am going to get some sleep," he says rubbing his forehead and getting up.

◆

As Tara predicted, it wasn't until the next morning when everyone was finally awake.

"'Morning guys!" says Sameer as he walks into the living room. "Hangover *utra*?"

"Abbey yaar! Won't even let me sleep in peace," mumbles Akshay.

"You guys have been sleeping for more than twenty hours! Aur kitna?" says Sameer. "It's ten in the morning. Let's grab some breakfast, yaar. I'm very hungry."

"Where is Preeti?" asks Gurav.

"She must be in her apartment... let me get her, you guys freshen up. We will go to Appu's for breakfast," says Sameer.

◆

"*Bhaiyya, teen bun maska, chaar bread omelette, paanch chai...*" Tara places the order at the makeshift eating joint by the road.

"Did she tell you guys something?" asks Sameer after failing to connect to Preeti's number.

"You were the last person to see her yesterday... no?" says Akshay.

"Call her?" Nivi suggests.

"Of course, I have... like a thousand times. Her phone is off the grid!" Sameer says.

"Is everything all right? I mean it's not that big a deal, right? She might have gone out for shopping or maybe some work at the office..." says Gurav.

"Yeah, yeah, of course," says Sameer, pushing away the nagging doubt at the back of his mind.

◆

10/4/2014

Divesh mamaji is no longer amongst us. When mama called me that evening and told me that mamaji had passed away, I felt so terribly guilty that only a couple of hours before, I had been in bed with Sameer.

Mamaji's death has shattered mama. I don't think it has sunk in yet. He was her backbone and he is no longer here. I know exactly what she's going through right now. At least papa is somewhat better now, thank god.

The past few days have been a blur. Perhaps it is selfish on my part to think about Sameer right now, but try as I may, I can't stop myself. I refuse to believe that it was just something we did while we were high. Or was it? At least not for me... I want to talk to him, ask him why he had never mentioned Revathy before... why he does not live with her... I refuse to believe that he tried to hide it intentionally... maybe he does not love her anymore, but he does, obviously. Why else would he take her name... and that too during an act that is supposed to be sacred.

I keep struggling with these conflicting emotions – one moment I feel disgust and betrayal, and the next a small portion of my heart tries to justify what he said and did. I can't believe Sameer would ever wrong me, but it's obvious that he did. Why else wouldn't he even try and contact me? Not that I want him to. Ever. A feeling of disgust crawls over my skin and I try to rub it off. I know this feeling from a long time ago. I wish I didn't have to go through it all over again.

◆

Sameer is pacing his living room restlessly, cellphone in hand, staring at Preeti's number on the screen. He is contemplating whether he should call her or not. He has an important meeting the next day, but he can't be bothered about it. He has already looked at Preeti's apartment through the peephole in his door over a dozen times in the last half an hour, hoping she'll turn up. It has been a little over a week and he still has no idea where she is and how she's doing. He has contacted her colleagues from office, but they don't have any idea of her whereabouts either.

Sameer flings the phone on to the couch. "What the hell, Preeti!" he says angrily. "You can't even call me? Or drop a message?"

I'm not going to call her now, he thinks. I have had enough of her drama. She acted so weird weeks before Holi and now this. I apologized for no fault of mine. Now what? Why can't she ever tell me what's on her mind?

His phone rings, breaking his chain of thought. Sameer lunges forward in excitement, certain that it is Preeti. The screen says it is Gurav.

Sameer lets out a sigh of disappointment. After a moment's consideration, he accepts the call.

"Hey, Sameer! 'Ssup? Any news of Preeti?"

"Hi. No, no news. Has she contacted you?"

"No."

"I'm sure she is fine."

"Yeah, of course."

"So... we are planning to meet the day after. There is this new gokarting place that Akshay was telling me about. It'll be fun. Chalega?"

"Nahi yaar, I will pass. You guys go."

"Why?"

"I have work," Sameer lies.

"Chal na yaar!"

"Nah! Won't be possible."

"This is thc third timc that you aren't joining us."

"I am sorry, yaar! I can't help it, too much work."

"I know you are lying, Sameer. You are upset that Preeti took off without telling you. Something must have come up at her end, I'm sure."

"No, I'm not upset."

"Sameer..."

"I gotta go now, have a meeting tomorrow. Bye!"

Sameer sits on the couch and starts browsing through the photos on his phone, pausing at one of Preeti and him.The photo was taken on Holi. His arm is casually thrown over her shoulder, and their faces and clothes are dyed in a riot of colours. They look inebriated but immensely happy. Sameer feels his anger dissipate as he looks at Preeti's face. Her radiant smile fills him up with happiness and warmth. After several minutes of staring at her photo, he finally switches off his phone.

Here I am, thinking about you like an idiot while you don't even give a fuck. Do you have any idea what I am going through, Preeti? The searing pain in my chest that does not let me breathe... it was all a joke to you, wasn't it? But it wasn't to me, Preeti. You are so much more than a neighbour. You are so much more than a friend. Only if you knew, Preeti, only if you knew!

◆

"Beta, it has been two weeks. I think you should go back to work now," says Aarti.

"No, mama, I want to be here for a little longer. Papa still needs to regain—"

"Beta,you know very well how uncertain everything is. You can stay here for another two months and he might still be as frail and weak as he is now,"says Aarti.

"But mama, after mamaji's death—"

"Yes, he had my back all this while, but now that he is gone, I will have to learn to manage everything on my own, Preeti."

"Still, mama—"

"Beta, you can't be here forever. I want you to live your life, think about your career."

"But—"

"Did we stop living after Hitu's death? *Nahi na?*"

Her late brother's name brings tears to Preeti's eyes.

"I'm staying for another week," Preeti says finally and walks away in a huff.

◆

14/4/2014

Mama wants me to resume work. How can I? After everything that has happened between Sameer and me, how do I go back to living in that apartment and pretend that nothing happened at all! 'Revathy' – the name rings in my ears all the time. God, how it stings and tears out the flesh inside me!

Even if I go back to Mumbai and move out of that apartment, I know I will always think about him. His fragrance will linger everywhere. The places we visited together will call out his name. There will be no running away if I go back. No, I am definitely not doing that. I am not changing the decision I made on the flight back home. There is nothing left for me there.

Sameer was a mistake, a big mistake I made in my foolishness. My skin crawls when I think about that afternoon. I was such an idiot!

No, I am certainly not going back. I will find a job here in Baroda. I will tell mama soon.

◆

It's a Friday evening and Sameer has just returned home after a long day at work. The moment he steps out of the lift, he heads straight to Preeti's apartment and sits on the stairs adjoining her flat. He has been working long hours for the past several days now, relentlessly trying to lose himself in work, only to discover that his grief is infinite. He has spent countless hours trying to recollect the events of the day he had woken up in Preeti's room. A nagging feeling at the back of his mind tells him he has wronged her in some way, which stops him from calling her again. He regrets giving her house's spare key when Preeti had misplaced the original one a month back and he regrets not searching the house for any additional note that Preeti must have kept inside her house before leaving. But then, he also knows if there was going to be a note, it would have been on the same paper that told him to close the door when he left her home after spending time with her, a time where he had no clue what transpired. And he had closed the door, it seemed, on all possibilities between them.

He feels miserable without Preeti. There's so much he wants to tell her – what he's done, what he thinks, what he's planning – but there's nothing he can do about it. Gone is the cocky confidence and the virile style people so loved in Sameer. Now he only yearns to see Preeti, to spend time with her, to watch the hours roll by effortlessly in her company.

No longer is he his jovial self around his friends; he is lost in thoughts that oscillate between blaming Preeti and himself for reducing their relationship to nothing. Sameer takes out his phone from his pocket and scrolls down to Preeti's number. He stares at it for several minutes and then finally dials her number. As he hears the ringing tone, Sameer's heart misses a beat.

"It's ringing," he says out aloud. "Finally!"

He starts imagining the conversation that they will have, wondering if he should sound casual or not. *I'm going to tell her that this is no way to behave with your best friend. Maybe not... maybe she is right... maybe I did something wrong that evening... I should ask her, she's the only one who knows.* His thoughts are interrupted by the beeping of the phone, indicating that the call is over.

Preeti feels a pain rise in her chest looking at the phone screen. Although she had deleted his number a few days back, she has not forgotten it.

I should have picked up the phone. I should have... no, it is better this way. I need to stand by the choice I've made. I need to forget about him and move on with my life. I just... I don't know... is it really so bad that I can't even speak with him? Yes, it is. He betrayed my trust. He does not deserve anything.

◆

21/4/2014

It's done now. My resignation has been accepted. Am I rushing into this? I don't know. Maybe I could meet him one last time before I leave Mumbai. It couldn't hurt, could it? I would want to meet the rest of the group too. No, no... what am I thinking? I'm not telling them anything. I won't gain anything by seeing him. He has given me nothing but heartache... of the worst possible kind.

◆

8/5/2014

Didn't expect to be so swamped with work in the very first week of joining my new office here in Baroda. Maybe it's for the best… the less time I have to think about him, the better.

He called me the day before yesterday. I didn't pick up the phone. What does he want from me now? He has taken everything away from me – my love, my trust, my self respect… I will never get over what he did to me. I want to be left alone in my misery. Loneliness is the only worthy companion, I have come to realize.

◆

Sameer lies in bed, wide awake. It's 3 a.m. He has been woken by a nightmare that lingers just outside the reach of his memory. Sameer picks up his phone and scrolls down to a number. He thinks about the times he would call her in the middle of the night.

"Hey!"

"Huh? Sameer?" Preeti said sleepily. "It's four in the morning! What in the name of…?"

"I was getting bored," he lied, not telling her that he had been woken up by a nightmare – the same one that always plagued him.

"What? Bored? Go to sleep, Sameer. I have to wake up early for office, don't mess around."

"I'm not messing around! I'm really bored!"

"God, Sameer!"

"Arrey, come over na!"

"No!"

"Please, I'm not going to rob you!"

"You aren't going to drop this, are you?"

"No," he said and laughed.

"Yaar!" Preeti grumbled.

Preeti went over to Sameer's apartment and they both headed upstairs, to the terrace atop the building. They sat in silence, their shoulders touching, not talking much but looking at the starlit sky. They were wrapped up in blankets, hot cocoa in hand, watching the Mumbai landscape that refused to go to sleep.

Sameer smiles at the memory – the unblemished beauty of that moment is now gone forever. He switches off his phone with a heavy heart, eyeing the wall clock and resigning himself to a silence that no longer appeals to him. Sameer knows that the only ones awake at three in the morning are either those who are lonely or those who are in love. Sameer is definitely lonely. He wonders whether he's in love.

◆

"How is she?" asks Tara as she takes a sip of coffee. She has come down to Sameer's apartment to meet him.

"I don't know," says Sameer, shrugging.

"Hasn't she called you?"

"No."

"Sameer, I know something happened between you two that day. I'm not going to ask you what. But whatever happened, she got hurt. Why don't you just call her and apologize and put it behind you? I know you miss her terribly."

"What rubbish!"

"You know it's not rubbish, Sameer. Do you remember that day when the three of us were smoking joints in your room and

I asked her if she likes you? I was in my senses when I asked her that question. I know that both of you love each other. It's so obvious, the way her eyes light up when your name comes up, the way your voice changes ever so slightly when you speak to her..."

"I don't love her. You know very well that no one can take Revathy's place in my life."

"Fine. But surely you love her as a friend... can't you just reach out to her for the sake of your friendship?"

"What friendship? She simply needed a support system around her, friends to fill the sorry void she had created for herself. I'm not reaching out to an immature, selfish person like her."

"Aren't you being immature too, Sameer?"

"Tara, that's enough."

"Sameer, you are making a mistake."

"So be it."

"Beta, you've been running around tirelessly since coming back from office," says Preeti's father as she places a jug of water on the bedside table.

"Come, sit here," he says, patting the bed.

Preeti settles down on the bed next to him while he puts away the files on his lap. "Haan, papa. Do you want something?"

"No, beta. Tell me, how is your new office?"

"It's okay."

"That's it? Okay?"

"Papa... it's just like the previous one. The same kind of people, the same politics – nothing new."

"But you seemed to love your previous job..."

"I did..."

"Then why did you leave it?"

"I couldn't work in the same office forever, papa!"

"But you don't seem to be very happy here."

"No, it's not like that... I will get used to it."

"Beta," he said holding his daughter's hand, "we've all been through a lot, especially you. Your mother and I have always been so worried about you... you deserved a better childhood... and now, you deserve a happy life, just like people your age. You moving to Mumbai was very painful for us, but we realized that it was for the best. We noticed a change in you after that. You seemed more cheerful, in fact, we had never seen you so happy before... but you seem to have gone back into your shell since moving here with us."

"Papa, it's not like that. I'm at a senior position now, so I have more responsibilities, that's all..."

"Beta," Pulkit says. "I've been bedridden for as long as I can remember and I've been missing for the most part of your life, but I'm still your father and I can see the pain on your face. It kills me that you won't tell me about it."

"Papa," says Preeti through the lump in her throat and wipes her father's tears. "I am very happy, papa... please dont cry; it really breaks my heart."

"Preeti, your mother and I both know something is wrong. Did you have a fight with your friends back in Mumbai?"

"No, nothing like that. I told mama the same thing too."

"Then what, beta? Are you tired of taking care of your father? Is that what this is about? Because if it is, I'll understand."

"No, of course not! Why would you say such a thing, papa?" she says squeezing her father's hands.

"Because I don't see any other reason for the change that has come upon you since coming here."

"Papa, I am overworked, that's all..."

Pulkit lets out a sigh of disappointment and shakes his head.

"You can talk to me about anything, you know that, right? Anything at all."

"Hmm," says Preeti, resting her head on his shoulders.

"Can I give you one piece of advice, my child?"

"Yes, papa."

"Don't shut yourself to the world. Don't ever doubt yourself. You did a lot of things that children your age would have run from. You have never let failure defeat you. You were a special child and will always be. Remember, life has its peaks and troughs, seasons that define its course. But most importantly, remember to look for the rainbow when it rains and for the stars when it goes dark. Never lose hope, my child... never lose hope!"

◆

3/6/2014

It is 2 a.m. and I can't get any sleep. Every time I close my eyes, he's here, right here, beside me. His warm breath filling my lungs, his skin brushing against mine... And then I see the want in his eyes – the want for me, the want for my skin, the want for my soul. He trembles, his universe shaken by mine... But then he takes her name. Her name. Not mine.

How could he deceive me this way? Sameer, how could you? Do you even realize what you've done? Do you even know the pain you've caused? Of course you don't. If you did, you wouldn't have done this to me. You might as well have murdered me rather than put me through this hell. The same demons I had overcome in my childhood glare at me again today, thanks to your lust. Tell me, how are you any different from the monster in school? Who is the lesser evil? I want to ask you all these questions. I want you to look me in the eye and answer them. But you sicken me so much that I won't. And it hurts because you meant so much to me.

I want to ask you so many things. Why is it so hard to get over you? I wonder if you too feel the pain like I do, the pain of knives stabbing me all over my body every minute. I wonder if you think of me when you listen to songs or see a place we have been to together or a thing we had done together, even if it's something as small as having a cup of coffee. Right now, I am overflowing with words I do not have and I don't know what I would do if I ever met you again.

I respected you. I loved you. You know how long it took me to find love, to find you? To overcome the fear of a man's touch? To know that love exists?

Do you know the worst part? That even when you have given me every reason to hate you with all my guts, I can't get myself to do it. I still love you. Damn it! Only if you understood, Sameer... only if you knew!

◆

'Cause baby you're a firework!

"Saale Akshay!" Gurav whacks him on the back of his head and says, "Why the hell would you play that song?"

"But it's Katy Perry, man! Have you seen her?"

"Yes," Gurav says drily.

"Like have you seen her..." he cups his hands on his chest.

"You guys have no decency whatsoever," says Tara and rests her head on Nivi's shoulder. Covering her face with a blue silk scarf, she dozes off.

Sameer is in the driver's seat, his lips pursed and eyes on the road. They are on their way to Lonavla for a weekend getaway. It was Nivi's idea. He is hoping to run away from the madness of being in his apartment and imagining that Preeti will show up.

"Abbey Sameer, have you taken a vow of silence? Like seriously... since the last one hour, you have been driving non-stop and haven't opened your mouth even once."

"Nothing like that, man."

"Sameer, seriously, is everything all right?" asks Nivi, "You have become very quiet of late..."

"Arrey nothing, yaar. I am fine. We have a long way to go, and I didn't sleep well last night... a little tired, that's all."

"Then let me drive!"

Gurav and Sameer switch places and the latter goes off to sleep, waking up only when they reach their destination – Sameer's bungalow in Lonavla. It's a two-storeyed building surrounded by lush greenery and a well-manicured garden.

"At last!" says Akshay, getting out of the car and stretching his arms. "Man, I love this place!"

It's seven in the evening and the skies have turned dark. There is a slight chill in the air, a welcome relief from the oppressive Mumbai heat.

Nivi wraps her arms around herself. "I can't wait to sit in front of the bonfire," she says, looking at the logs of wood stacked in a corner of the garden.

As Gurav and Sameer start taking out the bags from the vehicle, Ajay – the seventeen-year-old caretaker of the bungalow – comes running towards them.

"Bhaiyya! Let me take the bags."

"Ajay, how are you?" asks Sameer. "Where is *aai*?"

"She is making tea and bhajiyas for all of you."

Aai is Ajay's fifty-year-old mother, who once took care of the bungalow with her husband. After his death, she continued to take care of the property with her son. Sameer treats her like he would treat his mother and Ajay like his younger brother.

"How is she?" asks Sameer. "Is she taking her medicines?"

"She's great. I make sure that she does."

"Good," says Sameer.

They walk towards the main entrance of the house.

"Man, those bhajiyas, I can smell them from here!" says Tara.

"Seriously," says Gurav.

"Aai!" exclaims Sameer as he walks into the living room, where a squat woman in the *nauvari*, a traditional Maharashtrian attire, is busy laying out dishes on the table.

Her face lights up when she sees him. "Sameer!"

He runs to her and hugs her tight, just like he used to when he was a child.

"So much weight you have lost!" she says, running her hands on his face. "And these dark circles... aren't you sleeping well?"

Sameer simply smiles. "How are you, aai?"

"Fine, beta."

"Arrey, aai, we are also here," says Akshay.

Sameer's friends have come to this place several times before and have always received aai's warmth and hospitality.

"Kya, Akshay beta!" she smiles and blesses him as he touches her feet and hugs her.

"I can't wait to eat the bhajiyas you've made!"

"All of you, freshen up and come, the tea and bhajiyas are ready."

When they are back from their rooms, a bonfire is already crackling in the garden. They settle down around it, sipping hot ginger tea and eating onion bhajiyas.

"Aai, no one makes these..."says Tara gesturing at the bhajiya in her hand, "... better than you do."

"Thank you, beta! I am going to go now and get dinner ready."

"Thank you, aai," they say in unison as she walks inside the house with Ajay in tow.

The next few minutes are spent in absolute silence, interrupted only by the clanging of cups and saucers.

"When do we get the beer bottles?" asks Gurav impatiently.

"Not in front of aai," says Sameer in a curt tone.

"Chill!"

"Don't you ever use your fucking brains? That woman must have spent hours getting everything ready for us... show some respect!"

"Fine! I got it. Relax yaar!"

"Kya relax? Your pathetic little brain does not register anything easily."

"What the hell is wrong with you, Sameer? Why are you getting so worked up over such a trivial thing?"

"Sameer, calm down," says Tara.

"I am not talking to you, Tara."

"Sameer, I know you are still upset about Preeti, but this is no way to..." Gurav trails off as Sameer gets up.

"Do not take her name in my presence."

"Sameer, relax," says Nivi.

"I am," he shouts.

"Sameer, is this about Preeti?" asks Nivi.

"What the hell is wrong with you people? Preeti? How can any of this be about her? This is only about him," says Sameer pointing at Gurav, "being an asshole."

"Dude, enough," says Gurav, "I have heard enough of your bullshit. Don't take my patience for granted—"

"Or what?" Sameer laughs. "Haan? Are you trying to threaten me?"

"Sameer," says Gurav, walking towards him.

Akshay rushes to hold Gurav back while Tara rushes to Sameer's side.

"Gurav, don't," says Akshay, holding him by the shoulders.

"I'm not doing anything," says Gurav, shrugging him off.

"You wouldn't be able to even if you tried," says Sameer.

Gurav takes a deep breath and says, "Sameer, we have been friends for years. We have seen each other go through a lot. And we have always stood by each other, no matter what. And I am going to continue to do that... even now..." He puts his hand on Sameer's shoulder and continues, "Preeti left. And it has..."

"What did I tell you? Do not take her name in my presence." Sameer pushes Gurav's hand off his shoulder.

"Sameer, don't push me into doing something that I will regret."

"Calm down, Gurav," says Akshay, putting an arm over his shoulder. "Let's all be calm and rational."

"Usko bata, there's no need to tell me. He's the one who has lost his goddamn head after Preeti left him."

Sameer rushes towards Gurav with his fist raised.

"Sameer, no! No!" yells Tara, lunging at him.

"Come, let me see what you've got," says Gurav trying to push Akshay away. But Akshay manages to push Gurav further away from Sameer's reach.

◆

"Hi Preeti! How are things going on the Delta project?" asks her manager.

They are sitting in his office cubicle. It is ten in the morning.

"Quite good, Vinod. We are getting ready for the release two weeks from now. Everything is on track."

"Preeti, I have been very pleased with your work. Your dedication is commendable. And you have absorbed our work culture with unparalleled ease. Of course, nothing less would be expected from a person of your experience."

"Thank you."

"So, the reason why I called you is this... You do know that Indrani and Abhinav are supposed to leave for Malaysia in two weeks."

"Yes."

"Indrani's three-year-old son was hospitalized last night."

"Oh!"

"He has a congenital heart malformation..."

"Is he stable now?"

"No, not yet..."

"Hmm."

"We still need to send two people from Delta to collaborate with our team there. Obviously, Indrani can't make it now. Would you be open to the idea of taking her place instead? I know it's sudden... and given the situation at home..."

"Yes, Vinod. I need some time to think over this. Just one question, for how long are we supposed to be there?"

"For a little over a week."

"Okay."

"I don't want to rush you, but you will have to confirm within the next two days."

"I understand. I will let you know by tomorrow."

"Great."

Preeti spends the entire day in office distracted by the conversation she has had with Vinod in the morning. She does not want to leave her ailing father behind. But on the other hand, she knows the trip will bring a change of pace in her life and help her get out of the rut she's in. She is sick of Sameer and his memories, sick of being a prisoner to them. No matter how hard she tries to run away, zipping through the catacombs of her mind, she always runs right into him. He consumes her conscience with the lust of a prisoner behind bars who craves for freedom, clawing his nails at the walls in madness.

Later that night, as Preeti and her mother sit down for dinner around Pulkit's bed, a common occurrence in the Thaker household, her father starts a discussion that has become alarmingly frequent, much to Preeti's dismay.

"Beta, have you thought about marriage yet?" he asks his daughter.

"No, papa."

"Beta, you must! You aren't getting any younger... find a nice guy and settle down. Or let us know, so we can start looking..."

"Papa, I am in no hurry..."

"But we are, beta! Your mama and I are getting old. And with my health..." he takes a deep breath and continues, "I want to see you get married, beta. It will be the happiest day of our lives. We have had very few to begin with."

"Papa, I haven't met a guy yet who I would like to settle down with."

"How much longer?" her mother intervenes.

"Mama, please!" she snaps but quickly regains her composure. "I am leaving for Malaysia on office work," she says, her decision made that very instant.

"What? You are leaving for Malaysia? When? When was this decided? This is so sudden... I mean, it's great news, beta, but so sudden," says Preeti's father. "Did you know about this, Aarti?"

"No, Pulkit," says his wife.

"Papa, mama, I got to know today. I am leaving as soon as my visa is done," says Preeti and takes a deep breath, comforted that she won't be goaded about the subject of marriage for some time.

◆

"Sameer!" Tara knocks on the door of his room. "Sameer, can I come in?"

"Yeah."

It is 10 p.m. The bonfire has almost turned to ash. The dinner has been sitting on the table for close to an hour-and-a-half now. No one seems to be in the mood to eat. Tempers are flying high and egos higher. Tara decides to do something about it.

"Sameer, come, let's have dinner."

"I will in some time."

"Sameer, everyone, I mean everyone including aai is waiting for you to come so that we can have dinner together."

Sameer sighs and gets up.

"It was your fault," says Tara, looking straight into his eyes. Sameer opens his mouth to defend himself but Tara continues, "No, Sameer. Don't even try… it was your fault. Your reaction was childish and uncalled for. It wasn't Gurav's fault. If anything, he was really, really tolerant of your stupid behaviour. Had it been me in his place, I would have surely slapped you for speaking the way you did. I'm sorry to say this, but you've been acting like a jerk lately. Your anger about Preeti's departure—"

"How many times do I have to tell you that it's not about her?"

"Your denial won't change the fact. I don't know about others, but I will surely walk out of your life if you continue to act this way. I won't put up with your shit."

"I am sorry, Ta—"

She walks away before he can apologize, slamming the door behind her.

◆

"For your safety and comfort, please remain seated with your seat belt fastened until the captain turns off the seat belt sign…"

Preeti promptly reaches for the vomit bag again – her third time in the last hour. Abhinav, her colleague, gags violently and covers his mouth with one hand, the other lightly tapping Preeti's shoulder in a half-hearted attempt to soothe her.

"Thank you, Abhinav," says Preeti sarcastically, putting the bag away.

"Are you all right?" he asks.

Preeti nods and rests her head back.

Abhinav's gaze lingers on Preeti's face for several moments before turning away to look outside the window, a slight smile on his lips. He has had a crush on her from the moment he saw her in office.

"Thank you, ma'am! Hope you had a great flight!" says the flight attendant cheerfully as Preeti steps out of the plane fifteen minutes after it has landed at Kuala Lumpur International Airport.

She smiles weakly.

Preeti has had anything but a great journey. In fact, she is furious and quite miserable. To add to her woes, there is a further delay in the baggage arrival. By the time they collect it and make their way to the hotel, it is already late in the evening. Preeti spends the entire drive from the airport to the hotel sleeping.

"Preeti," Abhinav says softly and taps her gently on the shoulder when the cab comes to a halt.

"Huh?"

"We are here. We have reached the hotel. Come, let's go," he says.

"Yeah," says Preeti straightening up and flattening her hair absentmindedly.

"Do you feel feverish?" asks Abhinav as their make their way to the reception.

"I do actually," says Preeti.

"It's okay, just a couple of minutes, then you can rest all you want."

"Hmm... Abhinav, can you please take care of the formalities? I have to sit down, I'm feeling dizzy."

"Yeah, of course," he says and leads her to a couch.

"Can I get you some water?" he asks as she sits down.

"No," she says with great effort.

Abhinav sits down beside her.

"I am going to be fine, Abhinav. You take care of the registration."

"Are you sure?"

"Yes."

Abhinav takes off his jacket and gives it to her. "Be right back," he says and walks away.

"Good evening, sir! Welcome to the Grand Hyatt! How can I help you?"

"Good evening! We have two hotel room bookings," says Abhinav, handing over a piece of paper to the receptionist.

"Give me a minute, sir," she says and starts tapping away on the keyboard, her gaze alternating between the screen in front of her and the piece of paper that Abhinav has handed her.

"Sir, is your name Abhinav Mistry?"

"Yes," he says, taking out his passport in case she asks for an ID card.

"Mr. Mistry, our system shows just one room booked in the name of Abhinav Mistry, to be shared with Ms. Preeti Thaker."

"What? There must be a mistake. There must be a separate room booked in the name of Preeti Thaker. Could you please check again?"

"Okay, sir, let me check again," she says, tapping away at the keyboard frantically for several minutes.

"I am sorry, sir, but our system does not show any booking done in the name of Preeti Thaker."

Abhinav turns around and steals a glance at Preeti while she sits on the sofa with her eyes shut. "Can I have that printout back?"

"Sure, sir."

After looking at it for several minutes, reading and re-reading everything that's written on it, Abhinav says, "But it's clearly written here," he points at the piece of paper where Preeti's name is written, "that a room has been booked in the name of Preeti Thaker."

"Yes, sir, it does, but our system does not show anything."

"But that's the fault of your system, not our lookout," says Abhinav, his voice shaking in anger.

"Sir, I'm sorry for the inconvenience. We can provide an extra bed for no additional cost."

"I don't want an extra bed, I want a separate room!"

"I am sorry, sir, but there are no rooms available right now. We will have a vacancy tomorrow morning and we can shift Ms. Preeti then, but for now, you will have to share the room. There's nothing else we can do."

"This is bullshit! I have a confirmation for two hotel rooms in my hand," he waves the printout in the air, "and you are telling me that it counts for nothing. And now you are putting me in a situation where I have no choice but to accept what you're saying. Can I meet the manager? Because this is not acceptable at all!"

◆

"One more!" says Sameer, fidgeting with the glass in his hand, making the ice cubes go clink-clink.

It is a Friday night and Mazo, Sameer's favourite pub in town, is brimming with people eager to unwind after a hectic week. Sameer himself has had a long day meeting his clients.

"Scotch, neat," says a sharp, feminine voice.

Sameer turns around to see a woman in her late twenties, her long, dark, curly hair cascading down her back, her bare back peeking through the veil of her hair. Her light green eyes are as haunting as they are captivating; a fire burns in them. Her dusky complexion is flawless, her lips tinted with red lipstick, like cherries.

"Hi!" she says to Sameer and smiles.

"Hi!"

"Long day?"

"Sort of."

"Mind if I join you?"

"Not at all," says Sameer after a moment's contemplation.

"I am Samaira," she says, extending her hand after settling down on the bar stool next to Sameer.

"I am Sameer," he says as they shake hands.

"Haha, we've similar names!" she laughs.

"I actually had a date tonight... cancelled it last minute. It would have been my third date with him. I just don't connect with him, you know... he is a very nice guy, but there is no spark between us. It feels a little forced, like two strangers thrown into a situation."

"Hmm."

"I must sound terribly weird to you right now. We don't even know each other and I am blabbering away about random things."

"No, it's not weird at all," he says.

"Then why are you smiling?"

Sameer laughs. "Definitely not because I think you are weird, no, far from it... I was just thinking that the guy you were supposed to have a date with tonight must be cursing his luck right now."

"I suppose I can take that as a compliment," she says.

"It is supposed to be one."

"Thank you!" she laughs. "So..." she takes a sip of her drink and continues, "what's your story? What is a man like you doing all alone on a Friday night in a place like this?"

"Oh! I'm not sure... maybe I was waiting for you!" says Sameer, deliberately trying to suppress the heavy feeling in his chest, knowing he can prove his friends wrong.

"Ha!" Samaira chortles.

Sameer watches her as they talk. The way she taps her long, red nails on the sides of her glass, the way her long chandelier earrings swing every time she moves her head, her every move, her every gesture is magic, reminding him of the magic he once saw... in Preeti.

"So," she says, resting her elbows on the table, entwined fingers holding up her chin, "what agonizing ways has life come up with to haunt you like this?"

"Huh? Where did that come from?"

Sameer can't help but smile.

"I can see that something is bothering you."

Had she read something in his eyes? Or did his body language give somethingaway?

"Your eyes betray you."

"It's okay if you don't want to tell me," she says and takes a sip of her drink.

"There's nothing to tell..."

"Okay," she smiles.

They sit in silence for several minutes, sipping their drinks. There is a strange sense of comfort in Samaira's presence which compels Sameer to spill out the bitterness that has spread its tentacles through his conscience, the anger towards Preeti that is turning into venom and burning his insides. He thought he could swallow it, absorb it like every other pain he had come across in his life previously, but he had greatly underestimated this poison that was burning away his peace.

He wants Preeti, he knows now, not just as a friend, not just as a lover, but as everything she can be. But she doesn't want him anymore. Whatever had transpired that day had been enough to drive her away from him... forever. He can't let go of the fact that he wanted her. She was like a drug for him, better than any joint he had ever rolled. She was his addiction and he was struggling from the withdrawal.

He still feels angry thinking of how unceremoniously she has thrown him out of her life. He wants her to feel the pain he feels. He wants her to see the devastation she has induced, the trail of destruction she has left behind, the pain she has made him embrace in the name of love, which is threatening to destroy every inch of him.

He sees her everywhere – in the woman who stands in the corner of a room, in the stranger who walks past him on the streets. In every laugh, he hears her, in every tear, he sees her. Not a mere reflection – the complete *her*.

"I am sorry if I offended you," says Samaira, looking at the glazed expression on his face.

"Oh no, no, not at all..." Sameer trails off, shaking his head as Preeti looks right back at him, smiling. Sameer empties the rest of his glass and continues, "You know, I have to accept, I am slightly overwhelmed by your presence... you are incredibly beautiful."

"Thank you," she says.

"Care for a dance?" he asks Samaira, extending his hand out in front of her.

"I would love to."

◆

"Over here please, yes," Abhinav instructs the hotel staff as they bring in the bed.

Preeti sits on the edge of the bed, her face buried in her hands, fuming, the room spinning around her.

"Is there anything else, sir?"

"No, thank you."

After they leave, Abhinav sits next to Preeti and says, "I know this is very uncomfortable for you. I will do my best not to make the situation any worse."

"Hmm," she says without looking up, her eyes brimming with tears of frustration and anger.

"You should rest now…"

"Yeah."

"Good night. I will leave the lights on. I'm going to sleep over there, please don't hesitate to wake me up if you need something."

"Yes, thank you."

◆

"You," Samaira breathes laboriously, "are a brilliant dancer!"

"Thank you!" says Sameer as he pulls out a stool for her.

"You know," she pauses to gesture to the bartender that they need two drinks, "I haven't had as much fun before on the dance floor."

"I'm glad you did."

"You bet! Where did you learn to dance like that?"

The memories come gushing back. Sameer smiles through the pain. Revathy had taught him to dance. Revathy, the graceful classical dancer who could pull out moves from thin air, for whom dance was worship.

"Oh! I am a natural."

Samaira smiled. "I have had a great evening so far. In fact, one of the best in a long time. And it wouldn't have happened if I hadn't cancelled my date today. Everything does happen for a reason, huh?"

"Hmm... tell me something, the guy you were supposed to meet, what is he like?"

"You mean as a person?"

"Yeah, is he creepy or something?"

"What?" she chuckles." No! Why would you say that?"

"There's this guy who has been giving me dirty looks for some time now. I thought perhaps he's the same one you were going to meet."

"What rubbish!" says Samaira and laughs aloud. "You have an excellent imagination, you know."

"But I am serious! There really is a guy who has been keeping an eye on us for a while now..."

"Where?"

"Three o'clock."

Samaira steals a quick glance and turns around with a grave expression. The man in question is dressed in a floral shirt and tight orange jeans. His fake Ray-ban aviators sit on his greasy head. Sameer and Samaira sit in silence for a minute and then burst out laughing.

"Unfortunately, that's not the guy, no."

"What a shame! I will live to tell the tale."

"Haha..."

"Do you have to go now?" asks Sameer as Samaira checks the time on her watch.

"Honestly, I don't want to. It's just that I came here in an auto today as my friend borrowed my car for the weekend."

"That's okay, I can drop you."

"No, please, I wouldn't want to bother you."

"Not at all. It would be my absolute pleasure to spend some more time with you."

"It's done then, you are dropping me home."

◆

"Thank you, Abhinav," Preeti says through her stuffed nose as she takes the hot cup of tea.

"Did you sleep well last night?"

"Yes," she lies.

"I know you didn't."

Preeti lies in bed, covered in a blanket, a box of tissues resting near her. She's shaking with fever.

"This really sucks. I don't know when I'll be able to go see the work site here. And we are only here for a week..."

"Oh relax, don't think about office right now. You need to focus on getting better first."

"On top of that, this stupid hotel. They still don't have a room, do they?"

"It's alright. I'm going to find a hotel close by and book a room. You can stay here. I will shift."

"Thanks!"

"For what? Anyway, I'm going to leave for office now... I suppose you will have to work for a few hours..."

"Yeah, I will have to take a few conference calls, no way out."

"Don't overdo it! Just take it easy... please don't hesitate to give me a call if you need anything."

"Sure."

"And I will get a room by this evening, so don't worry about it."

◆

24/6/2015

Just a quick entry. Last night had to be, hands down, the strangest night of my life. And although Abhinav was a thorough gentleman, I couldn't help how I felt. I can no longer stay alone with any guy in a room. I didn't sleep a wink, afraid something would happen... I guess this fear will never leave me, no matter how old I get.

◆

"Yeah, right there, just around the corner," says Samaira.

As Sameer pulls the car into the visitor's parking lot, she lets out a sigh.

"What's wrong?" asks Sameer.

"I don't want our evening to end. Why don't you come up? We can have a cup of coffee... I make a mean filter coffee, by the way. And I also have a sea view from my living room."

"Ah, I see. Hmmm... let's go," Sameer says after a moment's thought.

"Fantastic!"

The first thing that Sameer notices when he enters the apartment is the distinct imprint of Samaira's persona. The décor is vibrant and bold, just like her. There are curious little artefacts all over the living room – a ship in a glass bottle in one corner, two huge tribal masks hanging from a deep blue wall in one part of the room and a Banyan bonsai right next to the window.

"You find it strange, don't you?" asks Samaira when she notices him studying the details of the room.

"Of course not! It's anything but strange. It's actually quite intriguing."

"Thank you! I've been fortunate enough to have gotten the opportunity to travel extensively, and I always make it a point to pick up something or the other from a place I have visited. Every time I look at it, it reminds me of that place."

"I can see that."

"Now if you'll excuse me for a minute, let me make you a cup of my home-brewed coffee."

"Can't wait!" says Sameer as he walks over to the window. He throws the curtains open. A strong gust of salty wind hits his face. Far away, he can see the waves dancing.

"I have spent countless hours sitting by that window, doing nothing but taking in the sight," Samaira speaks from the kitchen between the jangle of utensils and cabinets being opened and shut.

For a moment, Sameer feels as if he's back in Preeti's apartment.

"I would do the same if I stayed here."

"And my world famous filter coffee is ready," says Samaira, walking into the living room. She places the tray on the windowsill and sits there. Sameer takes his place opposite her. Sameer says, taking a sip from his cup. "You weren't joking, after all! This is truly the best filter coffee I have had."

"Told you!"

"Tch!" Samaira exclaims as her bun comes loose. She pulls her hair back, takes a deep breath and looks right into his eyes. "I have to admit, Sameer," she says pushing aside the tray and moving closer to him. "I find you very, very attractive."

Her hypnotic gaze arrests him and leaves him speechless.

"Sameer, don't you have anything to say?" she asks placing her hands on his thighs and bending over slightly, not breaking eye contact.

"Yeah... I..."

"I know you are attracted to me, Sameer. I know that look too well, and I have seen it all evening. What are you afraid of?"

"I am not... afraid..."

"Shh," she says. She throws her legs over his so that her dress breaks into creases and glides all the way up to reveal her panties. "Right here," she says, taking his hands and placing them over her waist. As Sameer's fingers touch her bare back, he lets out a sigh and takes his hands off her.

"What's wrong?" she says, almost offended.

Eyes closed, Sameer shakes his head.

"Come with me!"

"What?"

"Sameer, let's go inside," she says.

"I..."

"Let's go," she says, leading him towards her bedroom.

Sameer follows with unsure footsteps.

"This makes for a better setting, don't you think?" she says as she turns on the lights of her bedroom. It's just as eccentric as her living room. She turns towards him and says, "Sameer, take me."

He feels he has heard those words before, but he can't recollect when.

Samaira is about to place her pouty lips over his. Just then, something on the wall behind her catches Sameer's attention.

"Look at me, Sameer!" she says turning his face towards her. "You can look at the room all you want after we are done."

He feels the soft nudge of her firm breasts on his chest as the distances disappear. Sameer looks at her as she closes her eyes, her lips quivering in anticipation.

"Samaira," he says, stopping her.

She opens her eyes. "Sameer, don't think too much, this is going to be fantas—"

"Samaira," he says with a sense of urgency, gesturing at the wall he has been looking at for several minutes now, "that painting..."

Samaira laughs in relief. "I will tell you all about it later," she says, throwing her arms around his neck.

"No," says Sameer, gently taking her hands off him. He walks to the wall, towards the painting.

The landscape of the forest... the solitary figure... the circle of infinity... life and death.

He has not forgotten. He never can.

Samaira watches in disbelief, a part of her extremely annoyed. No guy has ever turned down her advances before.

"This painting..." starts Sameer.

"I got it from an art gallery... some upcoming painter... very promising... don't you think? Tell me later... now come back here."

"Hmm," says Sameer absentmindedly as he runs his hands over Preeti's signature at the bottom right corner of the painting.

"What?" she asks.

"Have a good night, Samaira," says Sameer as he begins to walk briskly away.

"Sameer, what happened?" she asks holding him by the arm, stopping him.

"Nothing."

She shoots him a questioning look. "Is there something about me you don't like?"

"You are perfect."

"Then?"

"You are not her."

"Preeti, you should have called me!" says Abhinav, putting a wet towel on her forehead.

He came back from office to find Preeti running a very high temperature.

"Hmm... I..."

"It's okay... don't talk now. I'm cancelling my reservation in the other hotel. I can't leave you like this."

"No, it's okay."

"For god's sake, Preeti. This is not the time to think about petty matters... you are in no position to take care of yourself. Once you're better, I will leave. I'm not trying to take unfair advantage of the situation."

"No... that's not what it is," she barely whispers.

"I am not leaving you. That's it," he says.

It's almost two in the morning when Abhinav finally gets up to go to bed.

"Sameer."

Abhinav turns around with a start.

"Sameer," says Preeti, waking up all of a sudden. She looks around,confused.

Abhinav rushes to her side. "Are you okay?"

"Hmm," she says, rubbing her eyes.

Abhinav sits down on the bed beside her. "Can I get you something? A glass of water, maybe?"

"No, thanks."

"You should sleep now..."

"Hmm."

"Do you want me to switch off the lights?"

"No."

"Okay. Good night."

"Good night."

Preeti covers her face with the blanket and weeps silently, biting her lips until she tastes the vile, metallic taste of her blood.

Abhinav aches to comfort her, but he knows there is nothing he can do. The walls around her are too high for him to knock down.

◆

"Are you feeling better now?"

"Oh yeah, absolutely... thank you," says Preeti. "I can go to office today. Finally."

"You don't have to, you know..."

"Nah, I want to."

"Okay. So... they have a room available now," says Abhinav and smiles awkwardly. "You don't have to put up with me anymore."

"No, it's not like that, had it not been for you—"

"Or get scared that I would do something to you."

"I am sorry..."

"No, I understand. My room is just down the corridor. 503. Give me a call if you need anything."

◆

26/6/2015

I don't know how I will ever repay Abhinav for the way he has taken care of me the last two days. And despite the way I behaved with him, he was so caring and considerate and kind. I didn't mean to be rude, but the whole situation was so awkward. Both of us sharing a room... especially when we don't even know each other! But that's what touched me the most. Despite being strangers, he took care of me. I guess it's true that not all men are the same.

It is also true... when you love someone, you become immune to the hurt they cause you. You don't love hoping to get something in return, you love because you have to. In its extreme form, it is a need to give, not a need to get. I know he likes me. I can see it in his eyes. I can see myself in his eyes.

◆

"Oh come on! Be a sport! It isn't as bad as you think, seriously!"

"Have you tried it before?" asks Preeti.

"No."

"Then how can you say that it won't be as bad as I think?"

"Don't you ever take chances? Like, what's the worst thing that could happen?"

"Can I take your order now, sir?"

"Give us a few more minutes, thanks," says Abhinav, fidgeting with the menu in his hand.

Earlier that day, Abhinav had suggested that they should take a break from hotel food and go out for dinner.

"You said we were going to try traditional Malaysian food," hissed Preeti. "You had planned it all along..."

"Yes, I had."

"You are shameless, you know that?" she says, giving him a dirty look. "And I am not having pig brain soup, no way in hell is that going to happen."

"Do you remember what you said to me yesterday?"

"Umm... that I owe you one?"

"Yes."

"Oh no! No, no!"

"Come on, Preeti! I am not asking you to finish the whole thing..."

"I am not forgiving you for this."

"Yes, we are ready to place the order..."

"Yes, sir."

"Two samong moo."

"Excellent choice! Your order will be ready in five minutes."

"Thank you!"

"My stomach is churning at the thought of it," says Preeti as soon as the waiter is out of earshot.

"Don't think about it, that's the trick!"

"Do you often try out weird stuff like this?"

"Oh yes!" says Abhinav with a gleam in his eyes. "Since my father is in the army, I grew up in various parts of India. My food experiments started when I was five. We were in Nagaland at that time. That was the first time I tried dog meat..."

"What?"

"Yeah."

"Dog meat? Are you kidding me?"

"No, I am not."

"What does it taste like?"

"It's similar to beef, just a bit more tough."

"Yuck!"

"What? It tasted quite good actually."

"What other bizarre things have you tried eating? I don't know why I'm even asking."

"Well, not as many as I would want... but chicken feet would count as bizarre, I think..."

"Eww! Why would you eat chicken feet?"

"For thrill... it doesn't taste as bad as it sounds. It tastes just like chicken, just a bit more intense..."

They stop talking as the waiter appears with a tray in his hand. "Samong moo," he says, placing two bowls on their table.

Preeti gags at the sight of the dull pink, squidgy mess floating in a clear broth.

Abhinav smiles indulgently. "This is going to be interesting," he says, "Let's begin!"

"I can't, Abhinav!"

"Come on now, don't be a wuss!"

Preeti takes a deep breath and says, "Okay! But we do this together, yeah?"

"Yeah. And, you have to eat a portion of the brain too, not just the broth."

"Hmm," says Preeti, her forehead wrinkled, staring intently into her bowl.

"All right then." Abhinav picks up the spoon. "We do this together, right?"

"Give me a minute," says Preeti and pokes the mush in the bowl with the back of her spoon. "Oh god, it is so squishy! Urgh!"

"Enough drama! One... two..."

Preeti scoops up a piece and some broth.

"... and..."

She closes her eyes and brings the spoon to her mouth.

"Three!"

She holds her breath, readying herself to gulp down the quivering mass.

"Preeti, don't just gulp it down!"

Preeti opens her eyes to see Abhinav chewing.

"It's not that bad, seriously!"

Preeti takes a bite.

"I'm not sure what this tastes like. It is...weird."

"Yeah, it's okay."

They sit in silence for several minutes, taking in one painful morsel at a time, hating each one just as much as the next.

"I am done," says Preeti after a few minutes. Her bowl looks just as abundant as it did when the waiter brought it to the table. "Can we just pay the bill and get out of here?"

"Okay," says Abhinav, not wanting to let on that he is just as eager to get out."If you insist."

"God! That shit was weird!" says Preeti the moment they step out of the restaurant."And I am never going on any food adventures with you, ever!"

"Yeah," he says.

"Yeah? That's all you have to say? You just made me eat a pig's brain! You... you swine!"

"Hmm."

"What's wrong?"

"Nothing," says Abhinav, sitting down on the pavement.

"Abhinav?" says Preeti as she sits down beside him. "Are you alrig—"

The next moment, Abhinav throws up violently. Several people pause in their tracks and look at him before walking away in disgust. Preeti controls her gag reflexes and pats his back.

"Urgh!" he says finally, his face still in his hands.

"Here, have a sip," says Preeti, offering him her water bottle.

"Thanks!"

"Hmm... well, no more pig brain soup for you!"

Later that night in the hotel room, Preeti writes in her journal.

28/6/2015

I hate to admit it, but I'm going to miss Abhinav's company once we are back in Baroda. He is such a weird guy! I wanted to laugh so hard when he threw up after eating that horrible soup. I still don't know how he managed to get me to eat it! It was surprisingly fun...

I have a strong urge to speak to Sameer today. I want to call him and tell him about the crazy little adventure I had. It's such a trivial thing. Why would someone want to call a person who has wronged them so immensely just to tell him/her about a petty experience that he/she had? I don't know. Why would he even want to know what I'm doing? I don't know that either. Maybe I will call him... don't know what I'll say though.

Preeti takes her phone and types Sameer's number from memory. After several minutes of rehearsing the conversation in her head, she finally dials it. Her heart beats furiously as she waits for the phone to ring. The call does not connect.

"Come on!" she mutters angrily. Tossing her phone carelessly on the bedside table, she goes off to sleep.

◆

"Two more days to go," says Abhinav as he eases himself into the chair and places his food tray on the table.

"Yeah," says Preeti, "I can't wait to go back... I am so sick of the food here. What about you? Does the food here make you... sick?"

"Ha ha! Very funny!"

Preeti bursts out laughing. "It really was." She wipes the tears that have formed in her eyes. "One minute you're bragging about your food adventures, the next minute you're trying to convince me that it can't possibly be that bad, and then you're throwing up right outside the restaurant."

"Rub it in, why don't you?"

"Jokes aside, I had fun!"

"Because I puked?"

"No, because of the experience itself. I mean, I'm not very adventurous, you know. I've never tried out weird food. I just don't do things like that. But I loved it! Even though I couldn't finish it..."

"I puked deliberately, to pay you back for what I had to endure during the flight," Abhinav says, sticking out his tongue.

"Yeah, right..." Preeti smiles, slapping him playfully.

"What else did you learn from our little adventure?" Abhinav asks, still smiling.

"Well, it did make me realize I should probably take some chances every now and then..."

"Nice! You know, I'm thinking about diving tomorrow."

"Diving? Where?"

"Sipadan National Park – the diving site there is one of the best in the world."

"I see."

"That you will."

"Huh?"

"You are coming too!"

"What? No!"

"You just said you wanted to take chances and be adventurous!"

"Yeah... but no..."

"Wait a minute, you can swim, right?"

"I can, sort of..."

"What do you mean?"

"I was ten years old the last time I got into a pool."

"Are you serious? But you must have surely gone to a beach or something..."

"I have, but I've never gone swimming in the sea..."

"I hope you don't mind my saying this, but you've been living under a rock!"

"That's a bit harsh."

"Of course it is! Why don't you make me take back my words? Let's go diving. I promise you, you won't regret it."

Preeti gives him a long hard look. "You've tried that trick on me already."

"And I'm hoping it works a second time too!"

"You're unbelievable!"

"Should I book the tickets then?"

Preeti's lips defy her will to keep a straight face and curl into a smile. "Not so fast... tell me something, why do you want me to come? Why is it so important for you that I accompany you?"

"It's quite simple. I want you to come because I like your company. I want an opportunity to get to know you better... as a friend," he adds."I think you are a really nice person, even with all the layers you hide under. And I also think that for some reason, you tend to arrest your freedom..."

"Have you considered getting into sales?" asks Preeti.

Abhinav bursts out laughing. "No, I haven't, yet."

"You do have a very convincing sales pitch... but how far is it from here? And how do we get there?"

"We will have to fly to Tawau from here. It will take us about two hours..."

"Wait a minute. Fly? No, no, no, this is not happening if we are meant to fly. Our flight is scheduled day after, Abhinav!"

"So?"

"Abhinav, do you remember what happened on our flight from India to Kuala Lumpur?"

"You threw up a couple of times, big deal!"

"I was in a bad state! And you could be a bit more sensitive, you know? It was a big deal!"

"Bit more sensitive? Me? Do you even hear yourself, Preeti? If there is anyone who needs a lesson in being sensitive, it is you! When someone takes care of you when you are ill, you should be grateful instead of thinking that the person is trying to take advantage of you."

"Why are you getting so offended?"

"I made a huge mistake by asking you to join me for a diving trip. Just forget it, okay?"

"What? I don't get it..."

"It's okay, just forget it," says Abhinav, picking up his tray.

◆

"Hi Abhinav!"

"Yeah, tell me," he says in a strict businesslike tone.

"Have you left for Tawau yet?"

"No."

"I just called to wish you a safe trip. I hope you have a wonderful..."

"I am not going."

"Oh! Where are you right now?"

"In my room."

"Okay. So... Abhinav, I want to apologize..."

"Forget it."

Preeti takes a deep breath. "Abhinav, I know you are angry with me. And you have every right to be. The thing is, my people skills suck. I don't always know what to say or do around a person. And I end up acting really weird. I don't have a lot of friends for that reason."

"Just let it be, Preeti."

"Please give me a chance to apologize, Abhinav."

"Go on."

"It usually takes me a long time to connect with an individual. But you... the way you took care of me when I was ill, that really moved me. I haven't come across too many people in my life who would do something for me without having any selfish motives. To cut a long story short, I don't want to miss the chance of having you as my friend. You really do mean a great deal to me. And the way I acted was way out of line."

"You do have a very convincing sales pitch."

Preeti laughs and says, "So, are we okay now?" The words sound familiar. And then she hears Sameer asking her the same question. For a moment, she freezes, lost in the wispy clouds of her thoughts.

"Yeah... hello... Preeti? You there?" Abhinav's voice jolts her awake.

"Yeah... you know, I was thinking, we should have another food adventure."

"Haha! I am up for it."

"Nothing crazy, though. I was thinking about heading to Petaling Street in the evening today."

"China Town?"

"Yeah."

"Sounds fantastic, see you then."

◆

"This place is crazy!" says Preeti as they walk under the blue signboard that reads 'Jalan Petaling'.

"The aroma of the food is just so tantalizing, I can't wait to try it out. Those dimsums look divine! Come, let's try it out," says Abhinav as he walks towards a food stall thronged by people.

"Hmm, give me a minute," says Preeti as she photographs the hanging red-coloured street lamps gently swaying in the wind.

"Two plates of dimsums," yells Abhinav over the din as Preeti continues to take photographs, simultaneously eyeing the stalls selling counterfeit watches and other goods.

"How much for this?" Preeti points to a pair of shoes.

"Preeti!"

Preeti turns around to see Abhinav holding two plates of dimsums in his hand, his white t-shirt soaked, beads of sweat rolling down his forehead.

"What the hell! Are you about to get a heart attack?"

"I might, you know. The people here are crazy! At one point, I thought the vendor was just going to toss the dimsums in the air and we all would have to fight until death to get our hands on them."

Preeti laughs as she takes a plate from him.

"Oh my god! These are fantastic!" says Preeti, her mouth full.

"Seriously! I should have got two more plates..." says Abhinav and turns around to look at the stall where he had been standing minutes before.

"Arrey! There is so much more food to try." She points to another stall. "I want to try those noodles. They look very tempting."

"Oh yeah! They do look quite awesome. You know...umm, I have been meaning to tell you something, I hope you don't mind."

"Not at all," says Preeti as she steps into a tiny space, which is a shop selling handbags.

"You Indian? You come from India? You speak Hindi? *Achcha daam dega tumko*!" says the shopkeeper.

"Abhinav, give me a minute!" shouts Preeti.

Abhinav gestures to say that she can take all the time she wants. After a few minutes, she steps out of the shop empty-handed.

"You were saying something, Abhinav..."

"Madam, okay, final price I give," says the shopkeeper, running after her.

"No, I don't want it!" says Preeti.

"Madam, I give you both bags for..."

"I said I don't want it!"

"Bloody... wasting time," the shopkeeper grumbles as he walks away.

"Let's try those noodles, what do you say?" says Abhinav, looking at a food stall where the vendor is busy tossing noodles in a wok.

"Oh yeah, absolutely!" says Preeti as they walk towards the stall.

"So... umm... I was saying..." he pauses to place the order and continues, "I was saying that you should never live with any regrets."

Preeti looks at him intently. "What? Where did that come from?"

"I'm just saying that life is too short... we should seize the moment, fix what is broken."

"Uh-huh," says Preeti.

"So often in life, we come across people who are very, very special," he steals a look at her. "If we are lucky, we forge beautiful connections with them. But life can be a real bitch at times and force us to destroy what we created. The important thing is to believe in what we created, to believe in the magic of the moment when we found those people in our lives, keep fighting until life bows down to our wishes and lets them be a part of our existence."

"You think so?" Preeti looks up.

"Absolutely."

"But what if those people were wrong to begin with?"

"If they were, you wouldn't be talking to them in your sleep."

◆

"Let's get something to eat," says Abhinav after they have collected their baggage at the Mumbai airport. Their return flight to Baroda is in four hours.

"I need to rush, actually. My previous society's secretary just called me..."

"Secretary?"

"Yes. I lived in Mumbai before. Didn't I tell you this?"

"Oh yes."

"Well... he insists that I clean the letters lying outside the door and pay the pending maintenance."

"Today? Didn't you tell him that you have a flight in four hours?"

"I did, but no use, the man is a little loony. Says he has to attend a family wedding in Nagpur and will be gone for a month, and besides, I was thinking of selling that flat, so might as well meet the broker who helped me find it and give him the key so that he can show it to prospective buyers. If not for this, I wouldn't have considered."

"Are you sure? Do you want me to come with you?"

"No, that's all right. Thank you so much, Abhinav! You have already done so much for me."

"And I will continue to, you know that, right?"

"Yes... I need to rush now."

"Yeah. Call me if there's any problem."

◆

"Namaste madam!" the security guard greets Preeti.

"Namaste!" says Preeti as she walks into her old building complex. The familiar sight immediately brings to her mind a fresh round of memories of Sameer and the times they spent together.

"You left the society no, madam?"

"Yes."

"Then? You come to stay again?"

"No, I have come to collect a few letters. Is Mr. Sharma in the office?"

"No, he is in his flat."

"Okay."

She goes to the building where Mr. Sharma, the secretary lives; it's just above her floor.

The elevator isn't working so she has had to take the stairs. By the time Preeti reaches the seventh floor, her upper lip is dotted with drops of sweat. As she catches her breath, her gaze falls on her apartment door. She smiles weakly as fond memories from her past rush at her. Absent mindedly, she picks up about a dozen letters, mostly promotional correspondence from various financial entities and a white envelope that holds her final settlement cheque from her previous firm. She puts the cheque in her purse and stuffs the rest of the letters in the exterior section of her travel bag. Then, as if on its own, her gaze travels down to Sameer's door. She can see that it is locked. And at the door lies a stack of newspapers. Preeti walks towards the door and picks them up; about six in all. She dusts her hands as she puts the papers back, wondering where Sameer might have gone.

After meeting the secretary, Preeti tries to make sense of what she has seen.

"Madam, secretary sir *mile*?"

"*Haan. Arrey*, you know Sameer, right?"

"Yes, madam… what happened?"

"Have you seen him today?"

"He not here, madam. He go with his big bike, got very big luggage at the back."

"Where?"

"Don't know, madam."

"When did he leave?"

"A week back madam, or maybe five days back… I don't remember."

"Are you sure?"

"Very much, madam. You can go and see for yourself, big lock on his door."

There is only one way she can solve the mystery. She pulls out her phone and calls Tara.

"Preeti!" Tara yells so loud that Preeti has to hold the phone away from her ears. "Where the fucking hell have you been?"

Before Preeti can answer, Tara goes on a rant, "This is so not done, Preeti! You just disappeared! You didn't even bother to contact any one of us. And I must have tried calling you a million times. So did Gurav. And Akshay. And Nivi."

"I want to meet you Tara, right now."

"Where?"

"In my old society."

"You're back?"

"How soon can you come here?" she asks, ignoring her question.

"Fifteen minutes, I am in the neighbourhood."

"Okay. I will be at Bareto's."

◆

"I am still angry with you, Preeti. Very, very angry."

"I am sorry, Tara. I know it was not the right thing to do..."

"You bet it wasn't. Just because you and Sameer had a problem, you severed ties with the rest of us. That's not what friends do, Preeti. Come to think of it, I feel Sameer was your only friend. The rest of us didn't really matter to you."

"No, Tara, that's not..."

"Shut up, Preeti, just shut up! What you did was mean, and selfish, and downright rotten."

"Tara, please listen..."

"No, Preeti, you listen. Do you know how worried we've been? Even Sameer's behaviour has been off the charts. Both of you have been complete dicks to us because you can't sort out your shit."

"I am sorry..."

"Preeti, you acted like a coward. A goddamn coward! Quite frankly, I had decided that I would never see you again. You are not worth my time, you know. I don't invest in people who don't value my friendship. Don't you dare cry now! You don't get to make it look like you are the victim. Because you are not."

Preeti holds Tara's hands. "Sorry," she says through her tears.

Tara pulls away her hands. "And yet, when you called me today, there was something in your voice that told me you needed me. And I couldn't help myself... I know you have suffered. I know that something happened that day between you and Sameer, something terrible that made you run away!"

Preeti buries her face in her hands and breaks down.

"Sshh," says Tara, getting up and hugging her. "It's okay, Preeti".

"I didn't mean to hurt you, Tara. I, I didn't mean to hurt anyone. I..."

"I know. I'm sorry for being rude. I just... I just wish you had trusted me enough to share your grief with me. You shouldn't have run away from the whole thing."

"I was a fool," says Preeti wiping her tears.

"We all are, sometimes," says Tara and smiles warmly. "Should I get you something? A cappuccino?"

"Hmm."

Tara places the order and comes back. "So, how is everything?"

"Okay, I guess... I've joined a firm in Baroda, work is good... I've just come back from Malaysia today after a week-long trip. And papa is stable..."

"And how are *you*?"

"I'm okay... There's something I need to know, Tara."

"Go on."

"Rather someone..."

"Go on."

"Who is Revathy?"

Tara pauses. "He didn't tell you?"

"No."

"Is she the reason why you left?"

"I... no... umm, sort of..."

"Revathy is Sameer's late wife."

"What? Late wife?"

"Yes."

"I didn't... I had no idea..."

"She died during childbirth. Their child didn't survive either."

"I... Sameer never once mentioned it..."

"He's still struggling to get used to what happened. He still has nightmares about it. It's been three years now. She was his childhood sweetheart, and they got married when they were twenty-one."

"Oh!"

"They were very happy together. Then they thought about starting a family and things started to go downhill from there."

"Hmm..."

"For four years, they tried to have a baby. By the end of it, they had gone to every doctor, tried out every treatment. Sameer no longer wanted a child, but Revathy refused to give up; she tried alternative treatments, and even went to *babajis* when the doctors gave up. Sameer couldn't deal with his wife's obsession for a child."

"Hmm..."

"This put a strain on their relationship. But when it seemed like they weren't going to recover from the emotional strain, Revathy discovered that she was pregnant."

"Oh!"

"The bitterness that had come into their relationship disappeared. It was almost as if nothing had happened."

"Hmm."

"Sameer and Revathy were so happy. They spent months planning their child's arrival, spent hours thinking of names. But in the seventh month of her pregnancy, Revathy went into premature labour after an accident. Both mother and child died."

Preeti sits in silence for a few minutes. "I... I don't know what to say."

"Preeti, I won't ask what happened between both of you. But I can tell you this much. He loves you. I have seen it in his eyes. And I promise I haven't seen that look in his eyes in a long, long time."

Preeti can barely see anything beyond the veil of tears.

"It has been a struggle for him to get over Revathy. He didn't date anyone after her, didn't even look at another woman. I always tried to explain to him that he should give love a second chance, but he refused to listen. Until you came along. Of course, it wasn't planned. He just got swept away by the feeling. And I think that was his hardest struggle. To fight those feelings, to hold on to Revathy..."

Preeti buries her face in her hands and sobs.

"Preeti..."

"I made a huge mistake, Tara!" says Preeti. "Is it too late?"

"Are you are talking about Sameer?"

"Is it too late, Tara? I can't reach his phone. I need to talk to him."

"Preeti, you must calm down. Everything is going to be fine."

"How could I have been such a fool? How could I doubt him? How could I doubt Sameer?" Preeti talks to herself rather than to Tara."Do you know where he's gone?"

"He's left for Goa. And don't you have to catch a flight back home?"

"I will cancel the flight. I need to meet him right now. I need to see him right now."

"Preeti..."

"Tara, I love him! I have always loved him. And because of my stupidity, he's not in my life right now. And every moment without him has been torture," says Preeti wiping her tears.

"There's nothing you can do now but wait..."

"I can go to Goa..."

"And then what? How will you find him there? He didn't tell me where in Goa he was going."

"When's he coming back?"

"I don't know. He didn't tell me anything."

"But he must have told you when he's coming back..."

"No. He took his bike and left, saying he was going to spend some time in Goa."

"I'm sure he must have told someone about his plans."

"Preeti, he hasn't told anyone anything. He called me en route. It was very abrupt. It was almost as if he wanted to make sure that none of us would stop him or question him, you know?"

"Where is he going to go from there?"

"Preeti, are you not listening to me at all?"

"He did tell me once that he would love to do something like that... go away for a few months, just travelling..." Preeti mumbles, making Tara wonder if she even heard what she's just said.

"So how long is he going to be on this road trip?" she asks Tara.

"Preeti," says Tara taking in a deep breath, "I don't know..."

"Hmm."

"No, I have to talk to Sameer. I'm not going anywhere until I do that."

"Preeti, Sameer has left."

"Oh come on, Tara! You make it sound like he is never coming back."

"He is not!"

"Did he say that?"

"No, but it sounded like that. I know him."

"He can't do that," says Preeti angrily. "How can he just leave everything behind?" Then she calms down just as quickly as she got agitated and says, "There's no way he can just get up and leave. He left on a bike after all."

"Preeti, he hired movers and packers a week back, none of us had a clue… I know it's hard to accept…"

"There's nothing to accept, Tara. I know he is coming back."

Tara sighs.

"I need to find him. I will go to Goa. I will bring him back."

"Preeti!" says Tara and shakes her hard. "What are you thinking? What will you do going to Goa! You'll go to Goa and then what?"

"I will find him."

"How?"

"I'll call him. And if he doesn't take my calls, at least he'll take yours…"

"We've tried calling him so many times, but his phone is switched off. I don't think he wants any kind of communication with anyone. Look, whether he comes back or not, I know he will contact me. I'll persuade him to talk to you then, okay?"

"Tara, you don't understand," says Preeti through the lump in her throat. "I need to find him."

"I understand, Preeti, but where will you find him? All I know is that he left for Goa. For all we know, he might have left Goa already. Goa's not a small place. Where will you look for him?"

"I probably sound crazy right now, maybe I am… but I have to see him, even if it's the last thing I do. I'm going to go by road, that way there's a chance I might bump into him."

Tara lets out an audible sigh. "You're not going to change your mind?"

"No," says Preeti stubbornly.

"Okay, then I might as well help you. This is mad."

Tara pulls out her phone and looks for buses from Mumbai to Goa. "There's no way we can make it in time for the bus at six. There's one at eight. It will get you into Goa by 10:30 in the morning."

"Thank you, Tara."

"You must be exhausted. You should spend tonight at my place and leave tomorrow."

"No, I have to move fast. I don't know how long he's going to be there."

"Ok," says Tara, her businesslike tone conveying her disapproval. "Let me book this one then."

"Thank you, Tara! So... did Sameer not mention anything at all about where he was going in Goa?"

"No. But he did say he was going to meet a college friend there. I don't know anything about him. Just that... oh wait... I think I know someone who might know him," she says, picking up her phone.

"Hello, Akshay!"

"Hey, Tara!" says Akshay.

"Guess who I'm with right now?"

"Gurav?"

"Shut up, Akshay."

Akshay laughs and says, "I don't know, tell me."

"I'm with Preeti right now."

"What?"

"Yeah."

"Whatever, I don't care."

"Akshay, listen, I need to know something. You remember that time you were looking for a graphic designer?"

"For my start-up idea, yeah, the one that never took off."

"You remember Sameer gave you the reference of one of his college-mates who stays in Goa?"

"Yeah. Juan Mascarenhas. I remember quite well… he had almost agreed to work with me, but then he was charging too much and…"

"Do you have his contact number?"

"Yes, I do. Do you want it?"

"Yeah."

"I will message it to you right now. But why do you ask? Some graphic design job?"

"I will tell you later," she says. "Do you know where he stays?"

"Somewhere near Ponda in Goa."

"Do you know anything else about him?"

"I don't know if this will be useful or not, but he owns a spice garden there…"

"Thanks. I need to go now. Bye!"

"Bye!"

"Why didn't you let me talk to me him?" asks Preeti.

"Now is not the time. And he is majorly pissed off with you. Anyway, so… ah! There it is," she says reading the SMS she's just received from Akshay. "So Juan Mascarenhas is most likely the guy Sameer was talking about. I have his number now, maybe you can talk to him, find out when Sameer is coming over…"

"Yes."

"Let's go."

Preeti gives her a questioning look.

"To the bus stand. It is going to rain," says Tara, sticking her head from under the garden umbrella they are sitting under to look at the overcast sky.

◆

They are standing at the bus stop and it has started raining.

"Are you sure that Juan Mascarenhas' phone number is out of order?"

"Yes," says Preeti.

"But where will you go?"

"I'll track him down."

"I'm telling you, this is pointless, Preeti!"

"I must leave now," says Preeti as the bus driver blows the horn.

"Okay."

"You are pretty annoyed with me, aren't you?"

"No, I'm not, may be a bit," says Tara. "Travel safe. Call me if you need my help."

"Yes, I will."

Tara hugs her tightly and says, "I really hope you find what you're looking for."

"Thank you!" says Preeti, getting into the bus.

She finds her seat and watches Tara run to her car in the pouring rain.

As Preeti puts her head back on the seat, she closes her eyes, thrilled with the prospect of finally getting some sleep. The bus lights dim and soon everyone on the bus falls asleep.

◆

"We have reached Panaji," says the conductor, loud enough to wake her up.

"Huh?" says Preeti waking up and looking outside the bus window. She can't see anything except for the drops of water running down the glass. She grabs her bag and gets off the bus, running to the nearest sheltered spot.

"Excuse me," says Preeti to the man standing next to her. He looks like a local and her best bet. "How can I get to Ponda from here?"

"Right now? You can't. No rickshaws available. When the rain stops, you'll be able to find one."

"Thanks," says Preeti.

She sighs and sits on the edge of a broken metallic chair. After waiting for almost an hour, the skies finally clear up.

"Rickshaw!" Preeti yells to draw the attention of the rickshaw driver.

"Ponda?" says Preeti when he stops in front of her.

"Okay, madam. Only seven hundred rupees."

"Seven hundred! I'm not asking you to sell me your rickshaw!"

"Madam, Ponda is very far from here. Thirty kilometres!"

"Don't you have a metre?"

"Madam, metre not working, but I tell you cheapest rates."

Preeti looks around and sees no other rickshaw in the vicinity. She's already wasted a lot of time. "Okay," she says and hops in.

"Madam," says the rickshaw driver, looking at her in the rearview mirror. "Where are you from?"

"Aah! Careful!" Preeti screams. Their auto just misses a head-on collision with a mini-truck.

"Everything under control, madam! I have been driving for a long time," he says as he zips along at breakneck speed.

"Please can you drive a little slow?" says Preeti.

"Madam, relax, where you coming from?"

"Mumbai."

"Coming for long?"

"Huh? No, no."

"You get very big bag there."

"Hmm."

After half an hour of silence, he speaks again, "Madam, we are here in Ponda, where you want to go?"

Preeti looks around. Small shops line both sides of the road, interspersed with coconut trees. There aren't too many people on the road. In the distance there's a small church painted a gaudy lime green. "Umm, do you know any spice gardens around here?"

"Which one do you want to go to, madam? There are so many here."

"Can you take me to the place where the spice gardens are?"

"You want to buy spices? I will take you to best one," he says before taking a quick turn to the right of the church.

"Fernandes Spice Garden," Preeti reads the tacky board that stands on the edge of the road.

"Jose Spice Garden," she reads the next board.

"Is there a Mascarenhas Spice Garden here? Or a Juan Spice Garden?" asks Preeti as she realizes that the spice gardens are named after their owners.

"Don't know, madam. We will have to see," he says as he abruptly pulls his rickshaw next to a shop selling toddy.

"Mascarenhas Spice Garden?" he asks the shopkeeper.

The man shakes his head.

"Juan Spice Garden?" asks Preeti sticking her head out.

"Don't know… you tourist? You buy some good toddy?" asks the shopkeeper as he picks up a bottle and walks toward the rickshaw.

"No," says Preeti firmly.

"You try a sample, free of cost for you!" says the shopkeeper, sticking a bottle in her face. "Premium quality!"

"No, I don't want."

"It's free to try, at least try a little bit. You come to Goa and not try toddy?"

"What are you waiting for?" Preeti asks the driver, "Let's go!"

"You don't want toddy, madam?" the driver asks in all seriousness.

"Drive!" Preeti yells.

As the rickshaw flees the scene with a grunt and a bump, Preeti starts reading the boards again.

"Pablo Spice Garden. Rebello Spices. Pauline Spice Garden…"

"Mascarenhas Spice Garden! Wait! Wait! Right here! I will be back in ten minutes," says Preeti and takes her suitcase out of the rickshaw.

A young boy is standing near the main entrance. "Is this place owned by Juan Mascarenhas?" Preeti asks him.

"Yes."

"Can I meet him?"

"Not right now. He has gone outside."

"When will he be back?"

"Don't know. Maybe three to four hours."

"Do you have his number?"

"Yes, why do you ask?"

"Can you give me his number? I need to talk to him."

"No, I can't."

"Okay, can you call him from your phone and let me speak to him?"

"Umm… I don't know."

"It's urgent," says Preeti. "Please!"

"He will get angry with me," he says fearfully.

"Oh no! Don't worry about that. I am his friend's friend. Juan told me to call him once I reach. I will pay you for the call," says Preeti and opens her purse.

"Okay," says the young boy.

"Umm, are you calling Juan?" asks Preeti after a few moments of awkward silence during which he is fidgeting with his phone.

"No, you said you would pay…"

Preeti hands him a fifty-rupee note. The young boy quickly dials the number and hands over the phone to Preeti.

"Moses, what's happened now? This is the third time you've called me in the last two hours," a man answers the call, his tone menacing.

"Hi Juan, this is Preeti. I asked Moses to call you..."

"Who? Give the phone to Moses!"

"I am Sameer's friend... Preeti."

"What? Who Sameer?"

"Sameer Arora, from Mumbai."

"Who? I don't know any Sameer Arora."

"How is that possible? You are Juan Mascarenhas, right?"

"Yes, I am Juan Mascarenhas. And I don't know any Sameer Arora."

"He is tall and..."

"Stop wasting my time and give the phone to that rascal! He is getting fired today."

Preeti hands over the phone to Moses and walks away.

"Madam, so much time you took," says the rickshaw driver, "but I won't take any extra money from you."

"She said she is your friend's friend! That you asked to..." Preeti hears the young boy speak into the phone before the rickshaw leaves the scene.

"Where are we going now, madam?" he asks.

Preeti does not respond.

"Where are we going, madam?" he asks once more.

"I don't know!" says Preeti, hiding her face in her hands. "Just keep going straight."

"Madam, I am wasting fuel. To go straight, I will charge another two hundred rupees," the driver announces, bringing the rickshaw to a halt.

"What? You said seven hundred rupees to reach Ponda," Preeti argues.

"Yes, seven hundred to reach. But we're already here. So I charge you extra. Discount for you, madam. I don't earn anything out of it. I am a poor man with a family to feed..."

"Fine... I'll pay you the extra two hundred bucks... now drive!" Preeti shouts and the rickshaw starts once again.

Five minutes later the driver pipes up, "We go straight, madam?"

"Hmm..."

She looks at the signboards they pass.

"Still go straight, madam?"

"YES!" she yells.

Suddenly they come across a broken signboard bearing only a few letters, the rest of it erased due to weather and neglect. "U-n-m-h-s garden," she reads aloud.

"Madam, we stop?"

"What for? It could be anyone!"

The rickshaw driver slows down. The longer Preeti looks at the board, the more compelled she feels to take a look. She stops him, and gets off, walking briskly to the gate. There's a man parking a bike near the gate. She decides to approach him.

"Hi!" she says.

The man turns around. "Hi. How can I help you?"

"Is this garden owned by Juan Mascarenhas?"

The man nods, taking a step towards her.

"I need some help, well..." Just then, she hears the autorickshaw engine start. She turns around to find the auto has made off with her purse and suitcase.

"My bag... stop! Thief! Thief!" Preeti yells as she runs after it. "Help! He took my bag. My purse! Oh my god!"

The man she was talking to moments ago runs after her. "What's wrong?"

"I left my bag and my purse in the rickshaw. Please help me!"

"Don't worry, we will get him," he says and immediately starts the bike next to the gate.

Preeti hops on the back and they begin to follow the rickshaw.

"I was such an idiot! I shouldn't have trusted him."

"Don't worry, we will get him," the man repeats, accelerating.

The rickshaw driver speeds up too, zigzagging through the road, avoiding potholes. But the bike catches up and soon they are a foot away.

"G-A-0-1," Preeti types in the digits of the rickshaw's registration number on her phone.

They are now driving alongside the rickshaw.

"Ae, stop!" says the man to the rickshaw driver.

"You rascal!" shouts Preeti.

The rickshaw driver looks straight ahead as if he can't hear them.

"Stop the vehicle now! We have your registration number, we will give it to the police."

Preeti clicks a photo of her bag in the rickshaw. "I have taken a picture of you with my bag and purse, you fuck-head! I am going to hand it over to the police now," she shouts.

The rickshaw driver throws a kick at them, but the man pulls away just in time.

"We aren't going anywhere without the bag. Stop or we will call the police!" says the man.

The rickshaw driver turns around and pushes the suitcase out of the vehicle.

"Stop! Stop!" says Preeti.

As they stop in the middle of the road to pick up the suitcase, the rickshaw disappears from view.

"Bloody asshole!" Preeti mutters as she picks up her suitcase. She opens the suitcase, takes her passport out, and tucks it in her pocket, along with her phone, which she is fortunately carrying in her hand.

"Let's go, we have to get your purse," says the man urgently.

"It's okay, let it be," Preeti says, sounding exhausted. "I don't have time for this right now."

The man looks at her in surprise.

"There was only money in the purse," she explains, "And I have more important things to take care of..."

"Are you sure? We could still go after him... or better still, file a report at the police station... you've got the number, right?"

"No, it's okay. I really don't have time for it right now. Could you please take me back to the garden? I need to speak to the owner – Juan Mascarenhas."

The man smiles at her. "That would be me."

"Oh! Oh my god. Wait... do you know Sameer?"

"Sameer Arora?"

"Yes..."

"Oh yes! Very well! How do you know him?"

"This is the Sameer I'm talking about," says Preeti, showing him a photo of Sameer on her phone.

"Yes! That's him," says Juan.

"He was supposed to stay with you, right?"

"Yes, but he never came here."

"Oh!"

"He was supposed to spend last evening at my place... but he called me late in the evening to tell me that he couldn't make it. Some change in plans."

"Did he tell you where he was going?"

"No... but he was calling from Calangute beach. I don't know where he is now."

"Do you have the number from which he called?"

"I think so," he says taking out his phone from his pocket. Preeti waits as he scrolls down the list of recent calls

"Here you go... He made this call from a payphone, I think."

"Okay," says Preeti, saving the number on her phone. "Let me make a quick call."

"Sure."

She dials the number.

"Hello?"

"Haan?" a rough, female voice answers the call.

"I got a call from this number yesterday..."

"So?"

"Can you tell me where your shop is exactly?"

"What for?"

"I'm looking for a friend."

"So?"

"Calangute to Panjim! Panjim! Bus going to Panjim!" Preeti hears the calls in the background. *The pay phone has got to be near the bus stop.*

"He called me from your booth..."

"Arrey, stop wasting time like that. What friend? What will I do if she called from Calangute beach? Go to police station if you can't find. How is that my problem?" She disconnects the call.

"What happened? Did you find anything?" asks Juan.

"Kind of... how far is Calangute beach from here?"

"A little over an hour."

"How can I get there?"

"Buses are available. There is a bus stop about fifteen minutes away. I could drop you there..." he says, starting his bike.

"You would? Thank you so much!" says Preeti.

"No problem," says Juan.

She picks up her bag and gets on the bike as they go back on the same road.

"So..." Juan says, "if you don't mind me asking, does Sameer not know you're looking for him?"

"No."

"Hmm."

"I know it sounds really strange," says Preeti.

"Would you mind if I ask why?"

"He is a friend. We had a bit of a misunderstanding some time ago and I stopped talking to him. I realized what a huge mistake I had made. So now I want to apologize to him."

"And it couldn't wait till he went back to Mumbai?"

"No, I don't think he's going back to Mumbai."

Soon they are at the bus stop. Juan parks the bike and leads her to the bus that will take her to Calangute. "That one will take you... and I think you should keep this," he says taking out three five hundred rupee notes from his wallet.

"No," says Preeti. "You've already done so much. How can I take this from you?"

"I insist. You have a long way to go, and you can't manage without money"

Preeti hesitates, but when Juan insists, she accepts. "Thank you so much, Juan! I will return the money as soon as I reach—"

"You worry about that later. You should board the bus now, it's going to leave."

"Oh!" says Preeti, rushing towards it, dragging her bag along. As she is about to climb in, she turns around and says, "I know that no part of my story made any sense to you..."

"No, it all did. Except for one thing..."

"Which one?"

"That Sameer is *just a friend.*"

A salty wind rustles Preeti's hair the moment she gets down at the Calangute bus stop. Without wasting any time, she starts scanning the place around her, looking for a shop with a pay phone. Sure enough, there's one right next to the bus stop. A heavily built woman stands behind the counter. Preeti swiftly walks towards her.

"I will have that packet of chips," says Preeti, having gauged from the phone call that the woman won't say anything until she buys something from her.

"Okay, what else?"

"That biscuit packet too..."

"Monaco?"

"Yeah... so umm, I got a call from your pay phone yesterday..."

"Didn't you call me sometime back?"

"Yes," says Preeti and pushes a five-hundred rupee note towards her on the counter.

"Keep one-hundred for you!" Preeti says.

"What you were asking, madam?" the lady asks, her tone suddenly polite.

"Did this man come to your shop yesterday?" Preeti shows her Sameer's photograph.

After looking at it for a long time, she finally says, "No, madam."

"What? But... but this is the number of this pay phone, right?" she asks showing her the number on her phone.

"Yes, it is. But if he came or not, I don't know. My elder son was here yesterday, not me, so I don't see anyone."

"Is he going to come today?"

"How I know, madam, if he will?"

"He is your son!"

"No, no, I mean, the man whose photo you showed me."

Preeti grits her teeth and says, "I want to know if your son will be coming to the shop today."

"Why, madam?"

"To ask him whether he has seen the man whose photograph I showed you," says Preeti slowly.

"I don't know, madam. He goes to college."

"Okay, thank you," says Preeti, walking away in a huff.

She looks around at the bus stop and takes a deep breath, wondering what she should do next. But before she can set out to look for Sameer, she decides to have some lunch. It's already two in the afternoon and she is famished. She makes her way to a restaurant on the beach.

"I will have the Goan masala prawns and one plain rice," says Preeti, selecting the two cheapest items on the menu.

"Would you like a drink, ma'am?"

"A club soda maybe," says Preeti.

"Goan masala prawns, one plain rice and a club soda, right, ma'am?"

"Yes."

As Preeti waits for her order, she starts browsing through the photographs on her phone to kill time. She pauses at one of

Sameer and herself. "How am I going to find you?" she murmurs under her breath, looking at the raging sea.

"Ma'am, your order." The waiter places the tray on the table.

"Thank you."

She places her phone on the table, Sameer's photograph still on the screen.

"Is that Sameer sir?"

"Yes, that is Sameer! How do you know him?" Preeti asks, surprised.

"He was here day before yesterday. Didn't speak much or anything, just sat here watching people try their hand at karaoke... but he gave me an awesome tip and chatted a bit about the weather, so I remember him. Customers like him are so rare!"

"Do you know where he is now?"

"No."

"Is there anything you could tell me about him that will help me find him?"

"I'm not sure if this will help... there was a problem with his bike. He asked me if I knew anyone who could fix it. I asked him to speak to our manager. You could try talking to him..."

"I will. Thank you so much!"

Preeti finishes her lunch quickly and rushes to the front desk to speak to the manager. His name is Jeremy.

"Did you enjoy the food, madam?"

"I absolutely loved it! I have a question..."

"Sure," says Jeremy.

"Have you seen this guy?"

"Yeah! What a coincidence!" He looks at Sameer's photograph. "And what a small world! This guy was here on Monday."

"He is a dear friend. Do you know where he went?"

"Yeah, I sent him to my cousin Barry's garage. He needed to get his bike fixed. I could call Barry and find out."

"That would be great!"

"But that idiot has lost his phone."

"Oh!"

"So you will have to go there yourself."

"That's okay. Can you give me the address?"

"It's not that far off, just fifteen minutes from here. Do you know where the bus stop is?"

"Yes, I do."

"Great! So there is a lane right next to the bus stop, keep going straight for about five minutes and you'll come to a sign that says 'Barry's Garage'. It's on the right side of the road. Tell him I sent you."

"All right, will do. Thank you so much!"

Preeti nearly sprints all the way to Barry's Garage. As she reaches the spot where she's supposed to find her destination, she notices the signboard that reads 'Barry rage', the paint chipped off the remaining alphabets. The creaking gate makes all the four men working on different machines turn around to look at her.

"Hi! I am looking for Barry. Jeremy sent me here," Preeti says nervously.

A thin, balding man walks towards her with a wrench in his hand. "Hi, I am Barry," he says.

"Hi! I am Preeti. I want to ask you something. Did a guy named Sameer come here two days back with his Avenger? Jeremy told me that—"

"Oh yeah, yeah! I remember that bike so well... very well maintained. Very few bikers take care of their girls as well as he has, smooth pick-up..."

"Hmm, yeah," says Preeti, feigning interest.

"Although I'm more of a *Harley Davidson* fan..."

"I see."

"I have one that's over thirty years old..."

"Nice! Umm, can you tell me something about Sameer?"

"Oh yes! I am so sorry... he took his bike yesterday evening."

"Did he tell you where he was going?"

"No. But I heard him talk to Amir there. He was asking about NH-17..."

"Where does that lead to?"

"It connects Maharashtra, Goa, Karnataka and Kerala," says Barry and shouts, "Hey Amir! Remember that guy with the Avenger?"

"Oh yeah! The quiet guy with the sweet ride!"

"Do you know where he was going?"

"No. But he was asking about the road conditions on NH-17..."

"Hmm," says Preeti, the disappointment in her voice obvious.

"This is important for you, isn't it?" asks Barry.

"Yeah."

"You could head to Karnataka... it's your best bet. He may be going to Kerala, but to do that, he will have to pass through Karnataka."

"Where in Karnataka?" asks Preeti.

"Most bikers head to Mangalore from here..."

Preeti takes a deep breath, unsure about what to do. Tara's voice rings in her ears, telling her that this is a futile exercise. Preeti thanks the men and walks out of the gate, heading in the general direction of the bus stop. She feels defeated, foolish for having thought that she could track down Sameer, embarrassed by the bravado that had taken over her.

"Panaji! Panaji!" a bus conductor shouts, drawing Preeti's attention.

She gets on the bus without much thought or question. From Panaji, she decides she will head back home.

Preeti spends the next forty-five minutes thinking about whether her failure to find Sameer is a sign that she should now close that chapter as their love had run its course. When she had made up her mind to find Sameer, she was convinced it was the right thing to do, and that finding Sameer would mark the beginning of a new phase in her life. Now she feels stupid for having allowed her imagination to run amok and give rise to thoughts that would never be realized.

At the Panaji bus stop, Preeti gets down and finds a seat on a bench next to an overflowing garbage bin. She decides to catch the next bus to Mumbai. She scrolls down her phone contact list and lingers on Tara's number, overcome by a desire to tell her that she should have listened to her. Although what she would really like is for Tara to tell her that she hadn't been foolhardy.

"Hello, Tara."

"Preeti? Hi! Where are you? Are you all right?"

"Mangalore! Mangalore!" shouts the conductor as the bus takes a sharp U-turn before coming to a halt.

"I am fine, Tara. I'm still here in Goa."

"Did you find him?"

"No," says Preeti in a small voice, "not yet."

"How much longer do you intend to stay?"

Mangalore! Last bus to Mangalore!

"Hello? Preeti? Are you there?"

"Hmm, yeah."

Mangalore! Last bus!

"I asked, how much longer are you going to be there?"

The bus driver blows the horn one final time before the vehicle starts moving, almost filled to capacity. Preeti feels the two remaining five hundred rupee notes in her pocket.

"Until I find him," she says, changing her mind in that moment.

Preeti gets up from her chair, drags her broken suitcase behind her and runs towards the bus that has already begun to leave. "Wait! Wait!" she yells.

"One ticket to Mangalore!" says Preeti breathlessly, managing to climb on.

The bus is a no-frills rickety ride – the legs of its seats have been eaten by rust, the foam of the seat cushions juts out in clumps like they've been clawed out by a vengeful cat. The ungodly scent of dried fish hangs thickly in the air. Preeti gags several times. She is amazed by everyone else around her seeming so relaxed and composed, oblivious to the foul stench.

As she walks towards the end of the bus to occupy the only empty seat, her stomach growls.

She notices a huge straw basket on the seat. It is covered, but she knows what she will find beneath the lid. The stench of dead fish is unbearable and she stifles a gag. A slight man with a thick mop of dark hair sits next to the basket, his hand thrown protectively over it. He grimaces when he sees Preeti, annoyed that he will have to place his basket on the floor because of her.

"Could you please move that?" asks Preeti.

He picks up the basket and shoves it under his seat. Preeti wipes down the wet patch it leaves behind before settling down. The stench is overbearing. Preeti tries to open the window, but it is stuck. Cursing under her breath, she wedges her bag underneath her seat, horrified that she will have to endure this for the next few hours.

Barely half an hour into the ride, fuelled by a strong fishy odour and a bus driver eager to mow down everyone on the road, Preeti starts to feel nauseous.

"Could you please move? I need to vomit," she says weakly.

The man does not budge. Instead, he stares at her coldly, then throws his head back and closes his eyes.

"The window won't open. Either you get up or I vomit here," says Preeti.

The man pretends to be fast asleep, pushing his knees further towards the seat in front of him to block the space altogether.

"What the hell is wrong with you?" she says angrily.

The man throws both his hands over his face.

Preeti searches her bag, hoping to find a paper or polythene bag. Her gaze falls on a sanitary napkin packet. She tears it open, spills out its contents in her bag and throws up inside the packet. She vomits several times. Her co-passenger is oblivious to her condition and is snoring loudly. Preeti considers various ways to dispose of the packet. Then her gaze falls on the straw basket beneath her co-passenger's seat. She bends down discreetly, pushes the lid off the basket with the back of her hand and throws the packet inside. Preeti straightens up and goes to sleep, feeling content.

It is almost ten at night when the bus stops for a short break.

"Fifteen minutes!" the conductor shouts.

Preeti wakes up with a start. Her co-passenger is missing and so is the horrible stench that's been bothering her from the time she boarded the bus. Preeti looks at the space below her co-passenger's seat: the basket is missing. Preeti heaves a sigh of relief and shifts her gaze to the space beneath her own seat. To her horror, her suitcase is gone. Preeti gets up and frantically looks under the other seats on the bus. As the bus starts filling up with people returning from the break, Preeti runs to the first person who boards it and says, "Have you seen a big red suitcase?"

"No," says the man before walking back to his seat.

"Have you seen a red suitcase?" Preeti asks the next passenger who gets on the bus: a middle-aged lady.

"No, my child. Why? What's wrong?" she asks.

"I can't find it. I kept it under my seat. I was sitting there," says Preeti pointing towards the back of the bus.

"You should inform the conductor if it's missing," she suggests.

"Yes," says Preeti under her breath and runs out of the bus to the tall, skinny man standing under a coconut tree and smoking a cigarette with a bunch of other men.

"Conductor!" Preeti shouts.

"Yes, madam?"

"Someone has stolen my suitcase. I think it's the man who was sitting next to me. He had a big straw basket. Tell me where he got down."

"Calm down, madam, your suitcase won't go anywhere. Please go and sit in the bus, I will find it." He takes a puff of his cigarette.

"How will you find my suitcase standing here and smoking a cigarette?"

"Madam, keep patience, I will handle."

"You find my suitcase right now or I will file a police complaint stating that you have a hand in the theft."

The conductor throws his still lit cigarette on the ground and stamps his foot on it. Preeti follows him. He boards the bus and declares, "Madam here has lost her..."

"Suitcase," Preeti completes his sentence on cue. "I have lost my red suitcase. It has a Malaysia Airlines flight tag on it... has anyone seen it?"

"There was a man with a straw basket who was carrying a red bag," says one of the passengers.

"Where did he get down?" the conductor and Preeti ask in unison.

"He got down right here!"

Preeti runs out of the bus and is followed by the bus conductor. He runs towards the shop in the corner selling tea and cigarettes. There's a small restaurant up ahead, but it is closed. A couple of vagabonds stand under the flickering light of the lone street lamp next to a dumpster.

"Did you see a man with a straw basket and a red bag?" Preeti asks the shopkeeper.

"No."

"Daddy," a young boy yells as he emerges from behind a tree, zipping up his pants. "Let's go home now, I feel hungry." He is wearing an oversized white T-shirt with six colourful handprints on it.

For a moment, Preeti stops dead in her tracks. The t-shirt makes her forget about everything. The next instant, she runs towards the boy and crouches in front of him.

"Where did you get this t-shirt?"

"Hey! What do you think you are doing?" yells the shopkeeper. "Stay away from my boy!"

"Where did he get this t-shirt?" Preeti asks the shopkeeper.

"I don't know. He was roaming near the bus stop yesterday and then came back wearing this. Told me some guy gave it to him."

"Madam, was this t-shirt inside your bag?" asks the bus conductor.

"No, but it's important to me... just give me two minutes."

"Madam, the other passengers are complaining, we should have left ten minutes back. First, you made a big fuss about your bag, now you are wasting time, asking questions about some t-shirt."

"I just need two more minutes, please. Who gave you this t-shirt?" Preeti asks the little boy.

His lower lip starts quivering. In the next few seconds, he begins to howl.

"Stop it right now, madam! And take your hands off my son," the man yells and steps out of his shop.

"I am not doing anything. I just need to know a few things, please let me talk to him," Preeti gets on her feet, her hands folded in humility. "Please, I request you. I will give you money."

"How much?"

"Hundred?" asks Preeti taking out the change left after buying the bus ticket.

"Ae, conductor! What are you doing for so long?" the driver yells.

"Madam, we have to leave now!"

"Five hundred!" says the shopkeeper.

Preeti quickly does the Math. She will be left with just a hundred if she gives in to the shopkeeper's demand. She hands him what he has asked for.

The bus driver blows the horn.

"Ae madam! We are getting late because of you!" A passenger sticks his head out of the bus window and yells.

"What nonsense is this! Why do we all have to wait because of one passenger?" shouts another woman.

"I just need two minutes," says Preeti.

"You have already taken too much time, madam. Either board the bus right now or we will leave."

"Beta, who gave you this t-shirt?" Preeti asks the little boy sweetly.

"Who gave you this t-shirt, Amit?" asks the boy's father.

"Beta, I will give you a chocolate... nice foreign chocolates." Preeti takes out a toffee from her pocket.

"Chalo bhai, this drama is going to take a long time," yells one of the passengers.

"Just two more minutes, please."

The conductor gets on the bus and says, "Madam, we have to leave now."

"Then leave!" Preeti yells in anger.

"Beta, please tell me who gave you this T-shirt and where?"

"Man on big scooter," says the little boy.

Preeti turns around for a brief moment to watch the bus leave, then turns to face the boy once more.

"Is this the man?" asks Preeti showing him Sameer's photograph on her phone.

"I don't know."

"Beta, please just look at it once," says Preeti.

"Don't remember," says the boy and starts crying again.

"Can you tell me where he was going?" asks Preeti. "This way or that way?"

The little boy points his finger in the direction where the bus left.

Preeti's heart skips a beat. *I am on the right track at least!*

"Daddy, come, let's go."

As the man and his son walk away from her, Preeti gulps. She looks around nervously. The area is almost deserted except for three men playing cards under the lamp post. Suddenly, she feels exposed, naked. All she has is her phone. She regrets not getting on the bus.

"Excuse me!" She runs towards the father-son duo.

"Now what, madam?" asks the man, annoyed.

"I need your help, please!" Preeti pleads. "I was going to Mangalore and the bus left. I don't see any other buses going now."

"What do you want me to do?"

"Will there be any more buses leaving from here?"

"Daddy, I am hungry," the boy whines.

"We will be home in another five minutes, son," his father consoles him and then turns to Preeti." There might be... there usually are... you will have to wait here."

"How long?"

"I don't know. Maybe half an hour, maybe two...."

"Daddy!"

"I can't wait here all by myself. It's not safe..."

"I can't do anything about that," the man says bluntly.

"Can I please spend the night at your place?"

"What? Are you crazy? No!"

"I have no place to go, and it isn't safe for me to wait here all by myself."

"That's not my problem."

"Please, I will give you money."

"I don't need your money. Go away, crazy woman!"

"I am begging you, those men there..."

The man starts walking away with his son, ignoring Preeti's requests. Preeti trails him. He turns around after taking a few steps. "What do you think you are doing?" he asks Preeti. "Why are you following me?"

"Those men have been looking at me. If you leave, I am certain that I will either be killed, robbed or raped. I need your help, please!"

"I can't take you to my house! I have my wife back home and my parents, my son..."

"Can you please wait with me till I find another ride?"

"That can take very long..."

"Daddy, I hungry!"

"Can you please wait for twenty minutes? If I don't find a ride by then, you can go, just twenty minutes."

He takes a deep breath and agrees. They sit down on a broken cement bench by the side of the road.

"Thank you so much! Thank you, beta!" Preeti gives the child another toffee, the last one in her pocket.

They watch as a few speeding trucks pass by. There is nothing else for the first ten minutes. It is almost midnight.

"I am sure someone will come along," says Preeti nervously.

The man doesn't say anything.

"Oh look! A car is coming this way!" says Preeti, getting up and waving her hand wildly.

It comes to a halt, much to her relief. The driver is a man with a bushy beard that falls to his chest. Even though it's night time, he's wearing sunglasses.

"You need a ride?" he growls.

"Umm, yeah," Preeti says uncertainly, there is no one else in the car except for him.

"I am heading to Mangalore, if you could drop me somewhere along the way..."

"I am going to Mangalore too. I could drop you there... it would be great to have some company."

While she talks to him, Preeti notices that there are no other vehicles on the road. She looks at her watch, only five more minutes to go before the man and the little boy leave. The three men standing under the lamp post have not stopped eyeing her since she got down from the bus. She makes up her mind.

"All right then, let's go," says Preeti, choosing the lesser of two evils. As she gets into the car, she looks at the man and his son one last time as they walk away.

"Do you want me to turn down the music?" asks the man in the driver's seat.

"No, it's fine. And thank you so much for giving me a ride."

"Like I said, I could use some company too... what's your name?"

"I'm Preeti."

"I'm Viraaj. Hope you don't mind my asking, but how did you end up all by yourself in this place?"

"Long story... I was on my way to Mangalore on a bus, got down here for a break, then got left behind..."

"What?"

"Absurd as it sounds, yes, that is exactly what happened."

"Hmm..."

"Do you mind if I ask you something?"

"Not at all, go ahead."

"Why are you wearing those glasses at night?"

"I am blind."

"What?"

He bursts out laughing. "I am kidding. Trust me, you don't want to know why I am wearing these glasses. If you found out, I'm certain you would want to get down."

"Okay," says Preeti nervously.

"Hmm."

They drive in complete silence for the next two hours. Preeti is sleepy but doesn't dare close her eyes. She is unusually alert and her body is tense.

His silence scares Preeti. She watches the road ahead, wondering what is going through the driver's mind. *Is he planning something?*

"You can sleep if you want," he says. "You don't have to be scared of me. Don't let my appearance fool you."

"I am anything but scared right now," she lies, clutching the sides of the seat tightly.

"Great," he says.

Another hour passes before Viraaj speaks, "I noticed you aren't carrying any bags."

"Yeah, my bag got stolen."

"Oh! How?"

"In the bus."

"The same one that left you behind?"

"Yeah."

"Was there any money in the bag?"

"No."

"So you have cash on you right now?"

Preeti gulps. "I do," she says slowly. "But not much. Just a few hundred bucks, that's all."

"Hmm."

She leans as far away from Viraaj as possible, pressing her face against the cold glass window.

After about an hour, Viraaj says something most unusual. "You must be a virgin!"

Preeti freezes. Trying to sound as calm as she possibly can, she says, "Could we please stop for a break? I need to use a restroom."

"We can't stop right now. There aren't any toilets here."

A long lonely stretch of road lies ahead of them.

Preeti shifts uncomfortably in her seat.

◆

At about five in the morning, dawn breaks, putting Preeti at ease for the first time in several hours.

"Where do you want to go in Mangalore?"

"Could you drop me at a bus stop?"

"Which one?"

"The first one that we come by."

Viraaj smiles and says, "Are you travelling for the first time?"

"Sort of."

"Hmm."

"Are you sure you don't want me to drop you elsewhere?"

"Pretty sure, yeah."

"All right then," he says, stopping his car near a crowded bus stop."Take care! Have a safe trip!"

"Thank you!"

Preeti is about to step out of the car when Viraaj says, "You wanted to know why I wear shades, right?"

"Umm, not now... no," she says awkwardly.

"So, funny story... I got my sclera dyed."

"Okay," says Preeti, eager to leave.

"You know what the sclera is, right? It's the white portion of the eye..."

"I see."

"So, I was in Hampi... and ended up doing acid with some hippies. I woke up the next morning to find this," he says and removes his sunglasses to reveal his eyes. Preeti feels the hair on the back of her neck rise in fear. His eyes are completely dark. She feels like she is like looking into the eyes of the devil. "I have to go now, thanks," she says, quickly leaving, relieved to have made it alive.

Viraaj waves and drives away.

Preeti settles down in the shade of a huge mango tree by the roadside and buries her face in her hands. Exhaustion from the last two days, sleeplessness and sheer frustration is finally catching up with her. She looks up, tears brimming in her eyes.

I can't give up now. Not till I find Sameer.

Despite the stupidity of the idea, she decides to show Sameer's photograph around and ask people if they've seen him. She can't think of any other way to track him down. But when she takes out her phone to do so, she finds that her battery has died. The charger was in her purse. "How much more, god?" she says bitterly. She decides to call Tara from a pay phone.

"Hello, Tara."

"Preeti? Hi! God! Where are you? I've been worried sick!"

"I'm fine. Tara..."

"But where are you?"

"In Mangalore."

"What? Mangalore?"

"Yes."

"Have you found him yet?"

"No."

"How do you even know if he's there?"

"Long story... I'll tell you later."

"But are you sure he's in Mangalore?"

"Maybe."

"Preeti, I just remembered, Sameer has a childhood friend in Mangalore..."

"Oh!"

"Yeah... his name is Clive, if I remember correctly, and he lives in a village called Atoo."

"Do you have his number?"

"No, I don't. But Sameer once told us a story about him. Clive's father was a pastor in a church there, a very famous church, I don't remember the name..."

"Hello? Tara? Are you there? Tara?"

The call gets disconnected. Preeti tries to call her a second time and then a third, but fails to get through. She hangs up and walks to a shop selling snacks near the bus stand. "Can you tell me where Atoo village is?" she asks the shopkeeper.

"Atoo? I don't know. No village like that."

"There is a famous church there..."

"No, don't know."

"Okay, thank you," says Preeti and walks to a nearby dhaba.

"Do you know where Atoo is? There's a famous church there..." Preeti asks a bus driver who is having a cup of tea.

"There is no Atoo village, only Attur village. The Church of St Lawrence is there."

That must be the one. Preeti thinks excitedly.

"Yes, that's the one. How do I go there?"

"Take a bus. The next one will be here after an hour."

"Thank you," says Preeti.

She decides to have a cup of coffee before the bus gets there. Up ahead is a small stall, a nondescript place by the roadside, sandwiched between an overflowing garbage bin that is being raided by a couple of cows.

"One coffee," Preeti tells the man behind the counter.

The seats under the asbestos shade are all occupied. It's so crowded that Preeti wonders if it's the only teastall in the neighbourhood. All the men turn to stare at her. Feeling conscious, Preeti takes her coffee and stands away from them, avoiding all eye contact. Just then, she spots an unoccupied table behind the counter.

Preeti starts making her way through the crowd towards the table, ignoring the stares directed at her. It's barely fifteen steps away from her, but the fact that she is both emotionally and physically exhausted makes the distance seem much more. She feels as though she's in the middle of a desert, stuck in a vast expanse of nothingness.

As she draws upon the last drop of coffee from the cup, she freezes suddenly. Is it a mirage?

Her memories zip in front of her eyes – haphazard, erratic. Is it too early to be happy? Or is it too late? Why won't her feet do her bidding? Why does her heart fail her now? Why does her throat feel so parched? Why do her eyes swarm with scenes she had suppressed for an eternity? Or was her mind merely playing tricks with her heart?

But there is no mistaking that thick mane of dark hair. That mole behind the left ear. Those handsome square shoulders. That shirt he had worn the first time they had met.

There is nothing distinctive about any of these things. But not to someone in love. Not to her. It could be anyone. But she is certain that it is not just anyone.

Preeti walks up to him, her breath in knots. Slowly she puts her hand on his shoulder. As he turns around and their eyes meet, she finally breathes. All the lines she had practiced, all those declarations she had planned to say to him when she finally saw him, dissolve on her tongue. She laughs through her tears, places the now empty glass of coffee on the table and says, "Hi! Do you have some coffee I could use?"

Epilogue

The party is lavish, that much he would give them. Not really a socialite, he avoided parties and kept an arm's length from events that had nothing to do with books, events where he would have to meet and greet people with that fake smile plastered on his face.

But he owed his presence to the lady who had come for the launch of his last book amidst torrential rains, at a time when most people on the guest list had backed out. He had never invited the lady, but she had come down to the book store anyway, umbrella in hand, soaked to the bone, listening in rapt attention as he read out a few passages from *The Other Side*, his last book which was also his first horror offering. She had sat down in the second row, meeting his eye when he looked into the crowd and clapping the loudest whenever the opportunity presented himself.

So it was only natural that when she came down after the reading to get her copy signed by him, he gave her a polite smile and thanked her for making it to the event. She introduced herself and gave him her card, telling him that she would add him on Facebook. And she did. The very next day. He usually avoided talking to strangers, but there was something about the lady that appealed to him and set free the extrovert hiding inside. She was quite a name in the art industry, he came to know, and she showed him some of her paintings in pictures. He was bowled over. As a connoisseur of arts, he knew a masterpiece when he saw one. And this woman could churn out masterpieces like it was child's play. He was sure of that. And it wasn't just that. He had found a friend online. A rare thing for a person of his nature.

His was one of the first names she sent out an invite to for the party at her home in the suburbs. She had him swear that he would make it, no matter what. It was raining when he left and he fought traffic, potholes and ignorant jaywalkers to reach her place an hour late than what was the designated time for the party to start.

The music is what hits him first and then the sight of the crowd. Rain or storm, no one was missing this party… that was for sure. He wishes people would spare the same thought for book readings. He grumbles a bit, picking up a glass of juice from the tray of the server who approaches him.

"Faraaz!" a voice shrieks, all the heads turn to look at him. He smiles, giving a nervous nod to the person who spoke his name, moving ahead to give her a light hug and the bouqet he has brought, careful not to step on the shiny pink gem-studded saree that she is so elegantly carrying off.

"Happy wedding anniversary, Preeti!" he greets her.

"Thank you so much, Faraaz. I thought you'd never make it," Preeti says, excited to see him.

"I had to, couldn't miss this one... after all I owed you one!" Faraaz winks.

"Haha, come...come... let's catch up over another drink," Preeti urges him forward.

"Sure... it's good to see you after long... you seem to be doing great as the next big thing in the art world," Faraaz speaks out his observation.

"My, my... look who's talking, Mr. National award-winner!" Preeti teases him.

"Haha, no. I'm just a simple writer who doesn't even get ten percent of this attendance at his book readings," Faraaz retorts, pointing around him.

"Oh, come on! Hey, you haven't met my hubby yet... wait. Sameer... Sameer... here!" Preeti calls out.

The tall muscular guy turns towards them. There is a bit of grey in his sideburns, but he looks impeccable in the black tuxedo suggesting his taste for finesse as he shakes hands with the writer while exchanging introductions.

"I'll just be around with Mr. Johar, dear... was a pleasure meeting you, Faraaz. Have heard a lot about you. We should catch up at length sometime," Sameer says with a warm smile.

"The pleasure is mine, Mr. Arora," Faraaz reciprocates the warmth.

"So what're you painting next?" Faraaz turns to Preeti after Sameer takes their leave. Both of them take their seats near the bar, Preeti gesturing for the bartender to refill their glasses, red wine for her and a Coke for her writer friend.

"I'm working on a concept... it's an abstract form... would love to know what you think of it... do come down to the next exhibition... it will be there, waiting for you!" Preeti promises.

"Ah, I see. I look forward to it then," Faraaz says, picking up the glass of liquid.

"Enough about me, what's new on the writing front? When's the next one out?" Preeti asks, taking a sip of the wine.

"Worked on this anthology called LOVE. It releases next month," Faraaz announces.

"That's beautiful! Congratulations," Preeti shakes his hand.

"Thank you," Faraaz beams.

"Knowing you, you would have already started working on the next!" Preeti gushes."

"Haha, I wish it were that easy!"

"No?"

"Still searching for that concept... who knows when the muse will strike!"

Preeti goes quiet for a second, growing serious.

"What happened?" Faraaz asks, quick to notice it.

"What if you found your story right here?" she asks him.

"Sorry?" Faraaz looks puzzled.

"I could tell you a story... you can pen it down, the way you do. It has enough of ups and downs – love, friendship, loss, regret, hatred – everything that a writer could ask for!" Preeti states, looking him in the eye.

"Hmm... you know, I get hundreds of requests like these every week, don't you?" Faraaz asks and immediately regrets hoping he had not hurt the sentiments of his host.

"Haha, I know, but if someone can write about it, it can only be you... you know, I have read a lot of big names and if I say that about you, then there must be something good in it for you too," Preeti smiles.

"Ah, flattery..." Faraaz says, sticking out his tongue. "Won't get you anywhere."

"Well, it's a fact!" Preeti maintains.

"I see, so is this a true story? The one you are talking about," Faraaz asks, finishing his glass.

"Yes, as true as it can get," Preeti answers with a smile.

"And give me one reason why I should write it," Faraaz prods on, teasing his host.

"Ah, there are several. You will know when you hear the story," Preeti says, gulping down the last remnants of her drink.

"Sounds tempting!" Faraaz says, looking her in the eye.

"So let's go upstairs, this is going to take quite a while..." Preeti gestures her guest to follow her, the pages of her life turning back, only to reveal themselves once again.

★★

Acknowledgements

No piece of writing is done in complete isolation, independent from people or things. There is always someone or something that inspires you, motivates you and makes you channel the writer within. There are always people or things on your mind when you write, people or things that make your writing taste the fruit of completion. And these are the people I wish to thank for shaping the words that you read in this book.

I wish to thank my parents, Sadruddin and Hanifa Kazi for always encouraging the writer in me. The most special kind of thanks to Afreen, my partner in crime, and my closest friend, Ismail, for their love and support for all that I have faced in life – for shaping the writer in me. This part would also be incomplete without thanking my mentors and friends – Tuhin Sinha, Vivek Banerjee, Brijesh Singh, Ajay Pandey and Preeti Singh. A deep thank you to Rouble Nagi for sharing insights of her life as an artist. This part also makes me remember a late friend, Gaurav Tiwari of the Indian Paranormal Society, who launched *The*

Other Side in Delhi. I would miss seeing him for the launch of this one.

A special thanks to my editor and old friend, Stuti Sharma, and my dynamic publisher, Arup Bose for giving shape to this book and making it worthy enough to reach your hands. Heartfelt thanks to all my friends in the publishing and distribution industry who make sure that my books reach my readers.

And of course, the biggest thanks to Preeti Thaker Arora, the painter and activist whose life you have read between these pages, for trusting me with her story and believing in me to pen it down.

Last but not the least, thank you dear reader for picking up this story and giving my words a chance to fascinate you. I look forward to connect with you on Facebook, Twitter and Instagram (all @FaruKazi)... after all, we too share a deeper bond – we too are *meant to be together!*